"He's getting away!"

He couldn't call for an ambulance without his phone, which still resided in the inner pocket of his suit jacket. He reached for Isabelle and his eyes focused on the rip in his suit where she'd been stabbed. Matt pulled the jacket back slowly, prepared for the worst.

Instead of blood he only saw fabric. His eyes lifted.

She pressed her hand on her stomach. "It didn't pierce me. Your jacket... Was there something in the pocket?" Her frown cleared as she pulled out his phone and wallet. Cracks radiated across the screen. In the center of the phone he could see the point of impact. If the blade had hit flesh... He gulped.

Her right hand reached for his wrist.

"Isabelle, you could've been–"

"But I wasn't. You saved my life," she whispered. Her eyes filled. "He got away with everything. My phone, my wallet, my tablet...it's all gone."

He squeezed her hand. "All replaceable." Unlike her.

Heather Woodhaven earned her pilot's license, rode a hot-air balloon over the safari lands of Kenya, parasailed over Caribbean seas, lived through an accidental detour onto a black-diamond ski trail in Aspen and snorkeled among stingrays before becoming a mother of three and wife of one. She channels her love for adventure into writing characters who find themselves in extraordinary circumstances.

Books by Heather Woodhaven

Love Inspired Suspense

TEXAS TAKEDOWN

HEATHER WOODHAVEN

HARLEQUIN® LOVE INSPIRED® SUSPENSE

Recycling programs for this product may not exist in your area.

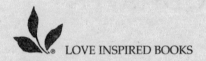

LOVE INSPIRED BOOKS

ISBN-13: 978-0-373-67824-2

Texas Takedown

www.Harlequin.com

Printed in U.S.A.

For where your treasure is, there will your heart be also.
—Matthew 6:21

ONE

Isabelle Barrows was hopelessly lost, caught on a winding path bordered by two wooden fences. Signs on either side read Pardon Our Construction. Without the six-foot-high fences, it would've been a pretty area with historic homes to view. Too bad she wouldn't see the result. She'd be back home from the conference within the week.

No wonder the walking feature in her maps application was considered beta because it'd led her on a convoluted route. The still tree branches that hung over the walkway offered her some shade. Sweat trickled off her brow. People had told her humidity in Texas would be intense, but she'd shrugged it off. She lived on the Oregon coast. She knew humidity, thank you very much. How wrong she'd been. Texas humidity was an entirely different beast. The air felt heavy against her skin.

Isabelle exited the app and pulled up a different map of the area. She had to be somewhere near Hemisfair Park and not too far away from San Antonio's River Walk.

A twig snapped. She glanced over her shoulder in the direction of the sound. A man in a dark gray shirt and black pants turned the corner. Isabelle smiled, but the man's steely gaze remained void of emotion as he quickened his pace toward her.

The fences designed to keep tourists safe from construction now seemed the opposite. How fast could she scale one if needed? She lengthened her stride and straightened her spine, hoping to exude confidence.

Her dad had taught her that criminals preferred to avoid confronting sure-footed people. Besides, maybe she misread the man's intentions, and he was just late for a meeting. Her neck tingled. But should she call the police on instinct alone?

Isabelle lifted her faux leather messenger bag off her shoulder and slipped it diagonally across her torso in case she needed to run or vault a fence. The weight of the laptop inside the bag pressed against her hip, but it wasn't enough to slow her down.

Up ahead the fences stopped, and the path opened into a park. She pumped her arms, no longer caring how foolish she might look to the man behind her. His breathing reached her ears. He was keeping up with her.

Not a good sign.

Another path intersected diagonally. Up ahead, waiting underneath the shade of a tree, a man in a brown shirt and tan pants straightened. Oh, good. A kind stranger who could help her if she needed it.

Isabelle offered a cursory smile. The stranger narrowed his eyes and strode toward her, exactly as the man behind her had done. A shiver ran down her spine.

She twisted and hustled in the general direction of the tourist area by the River Walk. No matter that it led her away from her own hotel. Her lodging was on the outskirts, away from the attractions. But right now, she wanted to be around people, lots of them.

In late afternoon at the end of August, the temperature and humidity seemed to keep everyone indoors. She scanned her surroundings and saw only trees, park benches and several other paths. Even a street would have been welcome at this point, but she had no idea which direction would lead her to one without taking time to look at a map.

The Mexican Cultural Institute to her left sported a Closed sign, or she'd have darted in there. The area opened slightly, but she was surrounded by more closed buildings on each side except for the stairs leading down, presumably to the River Walk.

She glanced over her shoulder. The men were side by side, walking behind her. They knew each other? Their eyes locked on hers as if homing in on a target.

She pushed off her toes and started to run. They followed suit. She was trapped inside her worst nightmare.

The memory of her dad's countless air-force lectures moved to the forefront of her mind. "You've crashed in enemy territory," he'd drill. "What's the first thing you do?"

"Establish and maintain communication with friendly forces, sir," she'd respond.

Isabelle held down the button on her phone until it vibrated, ready for her command. "Call the police," she shouted. Her fingers, slick with sweat, tightened around the phone as she pumped her arms.

Her hard-soled flats tapped on the steps. The thin guardrails lined the rock walls on either side of the curved staircase. It sounded like a stampede coming her way as the men's footsteps echoed off the rock.

She jumped the final three steps onto a thin sidewalk that curved along the water. Except this wasn't like the rest of the River Walk. It was an artificial cave formation. Stones the size of basketballs were placed strategically throughout the underground pedestrian area.

She sprinted along the canal, pressing the phone against her ear. "Hello?" She hadn't taken the time to press the speaker function. It didn't seem worth the two seconds of focus it would've taken her to find the right button.

A ringing hit her ears. "Pick up, pick up."

"What is your emergency?"

"Two men are after me." She panted.

"What's your location?"

The area resembled an empty cement cave that opened a short distance ahead. About a block away, another set of curved stairs led to a bridge and what looked like a hotel. "I don't know. A grotto-looking thing near the River Walk. It's behind a shiny skyscraper."

Her lungs hurt from the effort of sprinting and talking. She chanced a look. The men had split up. One man was on the opposite side of the water while the other was behind her. Up ahead, the two sidewalks converged. The truth hit her in the gut. If the man on the other side sped up, he'd be able to trap her. "They're gaining on me. Can't you use GPS?"

"Yes, ma'am, but the accuracy—"

Isabelle didn't take the time to listen. She dropped the phone into the front pocket of her bag but left it on. She couldn't keep up her speed without using both of her arms.

A few doors and glass windows lined the rock walls. She sprinted to one door, but it was locked. The rest of the windows were dark. All empty. She'd been told this was the slow season, but she'd had no idea it'd be deserted. Her throat burned as she pushed her legs to go faster. The man on the opposite side would beat her at this rate. Her flats barely stayed on her feet as her soles slapped against the concrete.

She rounded the corner and gasped. The sidewalks didn't simply merge as she thought she'd seen. She would be forced to cross a path surrounded by water to get to the other side, but she had no choice or the man behind her would catch her.

She ran into the middle of the path and froze. One man stood, hands out, ready to grab her, on the other end. The other approached from behind. And on either side of her there was nothing but water.

She was trapped.

The first assailant rattled off a couple of sentences to the other one in a language she didn't recognize. Her breath caught. What were they planning to do with her? The man in front of her pulled out a shiny knife. An involuntary shudder ran down her spine.

The memory of her dad sitting at the dinner table counting on his fingers played in the back of her mind. "Survival, Evasion, Resistance, Escape," he'd rattle off over and over. "Understood, Isabelle?"

She curled her hands into fists and widened her stance. She inhaled and pulled in her core muscles. The reality was, she couldn't fight two men at once. She glanced at the water. Diving without knowing the depth could be equally dangerous, but what worried her more was the laptop in her bag.

The flash drive doubling as a two-sided jeweled heart around her neck would likely survive with an overnight stay in a bowl of rice, but her laptop wouldn't fare nearly as well. She'd have come all this way for nothing when Uncle Hank was counting on her.

Her only other choice would be to leap diagonally to the tower of river rocks that held up the ceiling. Around the base of the tower, a rim of cement looked just big enough to get a foothold. If she made it to the tower, she could bypass the intersection of paths and keep going. She inhaled. Even if she made the jump, there was a chance her head would bump into the tower, a painful but not deadly possibility.

She sank her hand into the front pocket of her bag and twisted sideways so she could see both men at once. "Don't take another step." Her voice shook, but she could see the uncertainty of whether she had a weapon cross their faces. They remained on either end of the bridged path.

She took advantage of their momentary hesitation and backed up. It was now or never. She needed to soar like a ballerina over the water to the rock pillar. After three steps, she shoved off with her back foot.

Isabelle arched her back and stretched her right leg out. Her foot touched the edge of the cement rim. If she stopped now, her head would slam into the pillar, or she'd slip into the water. She twisted her hips and her left foot made contact for the briefest of seconds, pressing her into another diagonal leap onto the sidewalk.

Her ankle rolled underneath the awkward jump. The messenger bag hit the concrete with a decided crunch. She cried out and dared a look behind her. The men were both past the bridge behind her and were almost at arm's reach. Small rocks pressed into her hands as she pushed herself upright and sprinted, despite the lightning bolts of pain shooting up her leg.

Escape. She had to escape.

She screamed through the pain. "Help!" Her arms flailed as she pushed her stinging quadriceps to go faster, to keep up with the desire for speed. The sidewalk curved around another brick tower and then the ceiling disappeared. She squinted into the sudden sunlight. There… there in the distance, a boat with its motor running sat in the water.

A bearded man wore a pair of olive-colored overalls—a uniform of some sort. He looked up at her, confusion on his face.

"Help me!" She passed a trash can and flung it down behind her as she kept running. She doubted it would slow the men much, but every second counted. Would she make it to the barge in time? And would it matter?

Matt McGuire's heart jumped to his throat. The frazzled woman ran like her life depended on it. She was either mentally challenged or seriously in danger. Either way, he wouldn't be able to live with himself if he didn't try to help.

He boosted the motor and closed the distance between them. She glanced behind her and took a flying leap to the barge. She collapsed in a heap. "Drive," she cried.

At the sight of two men rounding the corner—one brandishing a long knife—he didn't need to be told twice. He reversed and sped away, pushing the barge to a speed he'd yet to try. He steered it at a sharp curve into the main River Walk loop. A police boat or officers on bicycles had to be somewhere for him to flag down.

The woman rubbed her ankle on the floor of the barge. She seemed okay, though. "Have you called the police?"

"Yes." Her breathing sounded heavy even over the hum of the motor. She kept looking over her shoulder.

"They can't get you now," he said. "So, the police said they were on the way?"

"Um." She pulled a phone from her bag and held it up to her ear. "Hello?" She frowned. "I can't believe they hung up on me. I couldn't run and talk at the same time. I thought they could use the phone locator to find me."

A few tourists walked past the shops and restaurants, but nothing was hopping yet. In a couple of hours, people would fill the walkways to bursting. "Their response time has gotten much better the past couple of years, but it still takes the police several minutes. I imagine the GPS thing isn't as accurate as we'd like to think."

She straightened. "I guess it's possible I accidentally hung up on them while I ran. I can't thank you enough for helping me. I think you saved my life."

While he kept his eyes forward, he noted in his peripheral vision that she seemed quite attractive when not screaming. And while her voice wasn't crystal clear over the motor, it did have a pleasant timbre and reminded him of a girl he once knew. "You're a tourist?"

"I'm here for a conference."

He nodded. At any given time there were between three and six conferences going on in the area. Late August was considered their off-season, but even then his hotel did well because the conferences never stopped. "For future reference, you probably should stick to the tourist areas. Outside the main River Walk, you can run into some sketchy characters."

"I never planned to end up somewhere alone. I blame my app." She shook the phone. "I'm going to call the police again."

Two officers on bikes zoomed on the right sidewalk in their direction. "No need."

He slowed the boat and stood, waving his arms to get the officers' attention. As they looked up, he anchored the boat to the side. It wasn't an official docking point, but it would serve his purpose.

The officer to the right turned his attention to the woman cradling her ankle. "Did you call about someone chasing you?"

"Yes! And one man had a knife. If this garbageman hadn't pulled over—"

Garbageman? Matt almost objected aloud.

He was the director of operations for one of the most successful hotels in the area.

The River Walk had its own cleanup crew and barges, but the hotel owned one to clean up their private nook, closest to its property. They needed the barge to haul the bags from the trash receptacles placed strategically around the grotto. It was especially useful after a conference or party, when litter inevitably made its way into the water. Matt hadn't wanted to wait for the usual waste-management rounds.

He glanced down at the overalls. He supposed it did look like he was a garbageman. But it was technically his day off, and since Louis had called in sick, Matt didn't mind filling in for his job. He always did what was best for the hotel. That, and since he had worked his way up to director, Matt had filled in for almost every position. And more important, he'd yet to train a substitute for Louis. Besides, what would he do with a day off? His family would arrive in a couple of days, and he wanted the hotel to look top-notch.

He had been testing the front-desk staff on new efficient task-management strategies earlier that day, which made it extra tempting to unzip the overalls to show he wore a dress shirt and trousers underneath.

The woman stood up and gave her account

of the men chasing her. Her animated expression complemented her wide hand gestures. Her brown hair hung in loose waves past her shoulders. The sides were pulled up by a clip, and thick bangs hung down over her eyebrows, the same way...

Matt felt his eyebrows rise. She looked just like Isabelle Barrows, his best friend for seven years in high school. That was, until he'd acted like an idiot. Her dad's post had moved across the country before they had a chance to reconcile.

But could it really be her? She wore tan dress pants and a white button-up blouse. Not something the Isabelle he knew would wear, but it'd been...what? Eight years? People changed, grew up, in that kind of time. He certainly had.

Before prom, all those years ago, Isabelle had confided an interest in Randy, the star quarterback. Instead of being a good friend, jealousy had reared up. Matt had warned Randy to stay away from Isabelle. But Matt hadn't stopped there, no. He'd proceeded to list all the reasons dating Isabelle would be a bad idea.

He'd never forget the moment Randy pointed over his shoulder. He turned around and saw Isabelle's wounded expression. The look of betrayal on her face had morphed into rage, and he never had a chance to explain he'd done it all because he liked her as more than a friend. Matt sighed, reliving the moment. What he'd done had been immature and wrong, but he'd been a kid. He was a different person now.

He turned off the idling motor. The breeze carried her voice, this time unencumbered. Yes, he definitely recognized her now.

The officer nodded. "Okay. Sounds like an attempted mugging. Maybe they saw you earlier take something out of your bag that looked valuable."

She frowned. "Maybe."

"We will keep a lookout for them, ma'am. In the meantime, I recommend you stay with other conference attendees." The officer looked over her head at Matt. "Can you drop her off at her hotel?"

Matt shrugged. "Sure. Where are you staying, Izzy?"

She turned her head around so fast he feared for her neck. Her eyes widened as her gaze connected with his. If he'd seen those eyes at first glance, the color of the deep blue sea, he'd have known immediately. He remembered staring into them while they talked for hours about everything and simultaneously nothing. She could make ironing sound interesting, discussing the cultural impacts the introduction of the iron made on society.

He smirked at the thought. "Hi, Isabelle."

Her rosy lips parted. "Matthew?"

No one, not even his mother, called him by his full name. Only his tax forms and driver's license labeled him as such. He had told everyone he much preferred to go by the shorter version, but he'd never told Isabelle. Truthfully, he liked the way she said it. Maybe because it made him feel like they had a special bond.

He blinked away the nonsensical thought as her expression shifted from surprise to hurt. His shoulders dropped. Great. She was remembering the incident.

She recovered quickly, though, as she pulled her shoulders back and smiled. "Wow. Matt." She nodded, as if processing.

The officer looked between the two of them. "So you know each other? Good. We have your number if we need to get in touch, Miss Barrows. Stay safe."

Matt made note of the fact she was called "Miss." Not married yet, then.

Isabelle looked at him with fresh eyes. "Wow. Matt."

"I'm not a garbageman," he said, waving at the outfit. "I—"

Her eyes widened, and she raised a hand to her mouth. "Oh. I'm sorry. Garbage person? No, garbage… Waste-management professional?"

He laughed. Same Isabelle, always quick to fix things. "No, I meant I'm director of operations at The Grand River Walk. Where are you staying?"

She told him, and he frowned. "We can't get there by barge. Let me park this at my hotel, and I'll take you where you need to go."

Confusion clouded her features, but she pressed her lips together and nodded. Maybe she didn't believe him? He tried not to think about it. "Hold on." He waved at a bar she could hold on to instead of sitting on the barge again.

It didn't take long to park in the small dock underneath the hotel's little cove. Isabelle stiffened at the dark atmosphere. "You're safe now," he said. He couldn't imagine what she'd gone through. Though he didn't really have that much time to start what could be a lengthy conversation. He'd do what he promised, though, and maybe even plan on grabbing a coffee with her sometime.

She followed him silently as he waved the magnetic strip on his badge to open the employee entrance. He escorted her through the glistening hallway to the front desk. "Ask Miranda to get you a hard copy of a map. She'll show you the safest routes to walk back to your hotel, for future reference." He placed a hand on her arm. "I'm going to change real quick."

She nodded mutely. Maybe she was going into shock? He darted into the employee locker room and quickly removed the overalls. From his locker, he pulled out a suit coat and an azure tie.

Not wanting to keep her waiting, Matt strode confidently into the marbled lobby. He smiled expectantly, ready to impress Isabelle, but he spotted only a tourist on one of the couches. "Miranda? I sent a woman here for a map."

"Oh, yes. I showed her how to get to the Adobe Suites. She left a couple of minutes ago."

"She wh—" Matt groaned. Could it be she didn't want to be near him for another second? Although, in his haste, he supposed he hadn't made it clear he planned to escort her back to her hotel. What kind of jerk did she think he was? "Could you pass me another map? Show me what route you told her."

Miranda handed it over. The Adobe, one of the cheapest hotels in the area, wasn't located in what was considered the tourist zone. She'd have to walk through a relatively sketchy area to get to it.

Would she be safe?

TWO

Isabelle studied the highlighted paper map in front of her. Perky Miranda at the front desk insisted there was a tourist-friendly way to walk to her hotel. Unfortunately, without going back on that horribly secluded path, it would add another half mile to her throbbing ankle. Besides, as far as she knew, they hadn't caught the men who'd chased her, so she decided to wait next to the doorman for a cab.

Why did her hero have to be Matt McGuire, of all people? Her eyes stung with unshed tears as the reality of her situation hit her. All alone in a giant city, after a near miss with armed men, she was left with a rescuer who had betrayed her friendship. Her hand reached for her collarbone as if her heartbeat was exposed to the rest of the world.

Matt no longer resembled the young boy she'd known throughout junior high and high school. His jaw looked chiseled, barely covered with a trimmed beard. The caramel mop with strands of honey-colored hair used to be bushy and unkempt, but now it was cropped, serving to emphasize his dark eyes. The man had aged well.

She'd grown up moving all over the country, aside from those seven precious years in Northern California. Matt had been her best friend right up until the day she'd stupidly listened to her girlfriends' advice: *"Tell him you like someone else, and then he'll finally notice you as more than a friend."*

Oh, he noticed all right, and Isabelle finally found out what Matt really thought of her. She had been on her way to meet Matt and confess her lie when she'd overheard him.

"Randy, look, man. You don't want to go out with her. Isabelle's... She's intense."

"I'm pretty intense," Randy responded.

"No, you don't get it. She has this way of questioning everything. And she's stubborn. You'll never meet anyone more stubborn. And so intelligent...logical to a fault, really, yet still somehow naive."

Her neck had felt on fire, and the heat had spread across her entire body, paralyzing her in the hall. Randy caught her gaze and pointed over Matt's shoulder.

Yeah, that had been a pretty bad day. Isabelle shook away the memories.

She glanced down at the colorful map. She'd been eager to check out the art galleries and historic buildings before the incident. Now sightseeing didn't hold the same appeal. She glanced up. Across the street, a man stood under the overhang of a building. He held a newspaper but stared directly at her.

The realization gave her an unnatural chill in the heat.

It was probably a coincidence. He wasn't one of the men who'd chased her earlier, but she didn't want to take time to study his face. She pretended to look at the map and dared another peek underneath her eyelashes. The man in the jacket continued to stare at her. Jacket? Who would wear a jacket in the heat of August? He reached into an inner pocket.

Was it a weapon? Isabelle no longer cared if she looked foolish. Her ankle smarted as she spun around to run back into the hotel and barreled right into another man. She screamed and stepped back.

"Isabelle!" Matt's hands grabbed her shoulders to steady her. "It's me. Are you okay?"

She flinched and twisted to look behind her. The man was gone. She pointed a shaky finger. "He—he—"

Matt let her go and stepped around her. "I don't see anyone." He offered her a kind smile. "You've had quite a scare today. It's understandable you'd be on edge. I'm so glad you haven't left yet. I never intended to leave you alone. Sorry for the miscommunication."

"Yeah, well, we've always been good at that." She stared at the empty doorway across the street. Matt didn't believe her about the man? Great. Where could he have gone, anyway? Behind one of the cars?

Matt stiffened. "Speaking of misunderstandings, I'd like to explain sometime about what you overheard me telling Randy all those years ago."

"No need. Water under the bridge."

He frowned. "What are you going to do tomorrow? Which conference are you attending?"

"The Oceanology Conference."

He pointed at the map in her hands. "Your conference is almost a mile from your hotel."

"I'm aware." She sighed. "Maybe I'll call a cab." It would have to come out of her own pocket, though, and the way the conference was split up, she would need four trips a day for the entire week. She couldn't afford it. The plan had been to walk everywhere...until those men had chased her.

Matt squinted as if deep in thought, little lines forming around his eyes. "If I weren't so busy—"

He felt guilty? "Matt, you don't owe me anything. It's not as if it's your town. You don't have to feel responsible."

He chuckled. "Well, I do. The River Walk has been my home the past couple of years. I'd hate for you to leave with a bad impression." He looked down at her feet. "How's your ankle?"

"Don't worry about me. I'll be fine."

A cab pulled to the curb. The doorman walked forward and opened the door for her. Isabelle got in and turned to give Matt a little wave, but he was already gone. Figured.

The other side of the car opened, and Matt slid onto the seat next to her.

"You don't have to—"

He smiled, the same smile that'd made her knees go weak when she was younger. "I promised those officers I'd escort you back to your hotel, and that's what I intend to do." His fingertips brushed her forearm as he leaned forward to point the driver in the direction of the hotel. The touch felt familiar, and a flash of homesickness hit her in the gut. She missed the boy Matt used to be. She blinked back the sudden emotion. It was unlike her to be overcome with feelings, but it'd been a most trying day.

The cabbie kept Matt occupied for a moment, discussing shortcuts and ways to avoid construction. When they'd run out of topics, Matt leaned back in his seat. "It's been a long time. Please let me take you out to coffee while you're here so we can talk."

"I told you, the past is water under—"

"Yeah, yeah." His eyes crinkled with warmth. "If that's true, then you'd have no problem catching up like the old friends we used to be."

Her guard broke down. He had a point. If she really weren't nursing a grudge like she claimed, he'd have been right. But she wasn't about to admit that his actions all those years ago still hurt. She forced a smile. "Okay. I'll check my conference schedule and get back to you."

Ten minutes later, the cab pulled into the driveway of her hotel. Matt hopped out and paid the driver before she could object. He opened her door and helped her out. "Today's my only day off, believe it or not. It'd be better to get our coffee on my calendar now. I'll walk you up to your room, and while I grab you some ice for that ankle, you can check." He caught her annoyed expression. "And then I'll be out of your hair."

She composed her features. "That's sweet. Thank you." Somehow he knew. He knew that the moment he dropped her off, she'd make sure she was too busy for coffee. Spending time with him after all these years would be more awkward than she had social skills to handle. But if they had something on the calendar, she'd feel bound to follow through.

They walked through the automatic sliding doors. The conference had proved engaging so far, but as an introvert, she craved some recharging time. Especially today. She'd never experienced fear as intensely as she had while running from those men. Would she no longer feel safe to go to the grocery store late at night? Or take a walk with her dog after sunset? From now on, would she imagine strangers following her?

Would she even be able to fall asleep tonight? She couldn't take any sleep aids like many business travelers did. She had a history of sleepwalking, and any treatments for insomnia would increase the chances. That was the last thing she needed in a big city.

"Izzy?"

She caught his concerned gaze. "Sorry. Lost in thought. Did you say something?"

"I was wondering if you knew off the top of your head if you were free tonight. Would you want to have dinner instead? I could wait in the lobby while you freshen up."

Did that mean she looked like she needed freshening up? She pursed her lips. If he thought she was primping for him, he had another think coming. But it didn't matter. "I'm afraid I can't. My research center is counting on me to network with potential investors." Responsibilities weighed her shoulders down. "I'm supposed to be at a dinner with other conference attendees in—" she glanced at her phone and groaned "—an hour." So much for time to decompress.

Her shoe caught on a snag in the carpet, and her ankle protested again. Matt put his arm around the back of her waist. "You really need to rest it."

The functional embrace was almost enough to make her forget everything he'd said all those years ago. A shock of heat slid up her spine. She remembered a time when Matt was nothing but sweet and caring. They had never run out of things to talk about. How many times had she gone home wishing he'd have shown a romantic interest in her?

"By the way, no one calls me Izzy anymore," she said.

"Oh? I seem to remember it was Belle in elementary, Ibby in junior high and Izzy in high school." He smirked. "What's left?"

Her cheeks heated at her younger self's insistence at changing nicknames all the time. "Just plain Isabelle, thanks."

"I thought you didn't like that."

"Yeah, well, that was for superficial reasons I've outgrown."

"Such as?"

Did he really have to push it? She sighed. "I feel safe, as an adult, from the joke."

"Joke?"

She felt her eyebrow rise. "Are you seriously trying to tell me you don't remember it?"

"Knock knock." His lips were fighting a laugh.

She simultaneously wanted to smack him in the shoulder and laugh along with him. "I knew you knew it." The rest of the joke played through her head automatically: *Who's there? Isabelle. Is a bell out of order? I had to knock.*

Oh, how she hated that joke and all the varieties that went with it. They had reached the back of the lobby.

Matt slowed. "Where to?"

She pointed to the left. Even though she'd requested a top floor, they'd put her on the bottom floor, where she could hear every footstep and door closing all night long. The smell of wet carpet hit her sinuses. The moisture was either from the heavy humidity or the remnants of a flooding.

Judging by Matt's tight lips, his hotel didn't suffer the same problem. She pointed at the door to the left. "This is me."

"Okay. I'll head for the ice machine while you get settled." The moment her hand touched the door, Matt's support left her. He strode down the hallway.

She pushed the plastic key into the slot, but instead of the little light turning green, the door opened, almost as if on its own. Strange. Had she not closed it all the way?

Utter darkness greeted her. Her breath hitched. She'd purposefully left the lamp on. Had housekeeping turned it off? She glanced at the door handle. The Do Not Disturb sign was still hanging where she'd placed it. Her back went rigid. Logically, it was possible the lightbulb had burned out.

She groped for the light switch but couldn't remember where it was. Her heart slammed into her chest as she searched for it with no result. What if someone was in the room, waiting for her? She jumped backward into the hallway, letting the door close in front of her. "Matt?" She hated the way her voice shook.

"Everything okay?"

"I think someone's been in my room." Her voice shook. He was going to think she'd turned into a basket case.

His long stride reached her in a heartbeat. "Are you sure?"

She shook her head. "No, but—" She waved at the door. "It's different."

His brow furrowed as he studied her. "May I?" He took the plastic key from her hand. The door opened easily as he stepped into the blackness. "Probably just housekeep—" Light flooded the room and into the hallway.

Her shoulders dropped. He'd found the light switch, which meant she had overreacted.

He spun around. Lines creased his forehead. "Izzy, call the police."

Matt couldn't believe his eyes. Every inch of her hotel room had been ransacked. The drawers weren't just open but pulled out of the dresser. The couch cushions and king-size mattress had been flipped.

The police directed him to wait in the hotel lobby as they interviewed Isabelle and the hotel staff. Isabelle iced her ankle in the chair perpendicular to him while they asked her questions. He pulled off his suit jacket. He could usually stand the heat and humidity in decent air-conditioning, but this hotel seemed to lack it.

Isabelle clutched her sparkly heart necklace. She shook her head to whatever question the officer had asked her. The jewelry looked bulky, almost gaudy compared to the elegance of her outfit. Frankly, it didn't suit her tastes. Or rather, the tastes she used to have. He didn't presume to know how much Isabelle had changed over the years.

Her manicured fingertips ran over the diamond-encrusted jewels on the left side of the heart. Fake, probably...he hoped. He cringed as he recognized the spark of jealousy. It would not rear its ugly head again. He was too mature for that.

As thick as the jeweled heart was, it was likely a locket of some sort...and none of his business. He would not ask her who gave her that locket. Although it might be part of the reason she hesitated to spend time catching up with him. Maybe she had forgiven him but didn't want to be alone with him because she was already attached to someone else. He leaned forward to catch a glimpse of her other hand.

Isabelle caught his movements and frowned as her hands dropped to her lap. No engagement ring. He smiled and pushed his arms out as if stretching, and her face relaxed.

The hotel staff gathered on the opposite side of the lobby. They seemed tense as they huddled. It seemed harder to believe the ransacking was a coincidence after the men in the grotto. Isabelle had thought a man had been watching her outside his hotel, but he'd credited it to nerves. Now it seemed like someone was targeting her.

The police officer stepped away from Isabelle. She took a shaky breath and smiled at Matt. "He said you're free to go. I'm sorry you had to spend your day off like this."

Matt watched the officers leave. "Did they have any leads?"

Her face fell. "Not yet. They're moving me to another room, at least."

"No. Absolutely not."

She pulled back, her blue eyes wide.

He sighed. He'd done it again, speaking without thinking. But it didn't mean his instinct was wrong. He stood. "You're not staying here. We've already discovered it's not safe. Besides, don't you have a sinus headache from these damp carpets?"

She blinked. "My allergies have gotten better over the years, but yeah, I've got a low-grade one that won't quit."

"I'll help you pack."

She flashed a smile that reminded him of all the nights he'd been tempted to kiss her. Some decent air-conditioning would be welcome right now.

"I appreciate your concern, Matt, but my boss already paid in advance for me to stay here. I can't afford—"

"My treat." There he went again. But he wasn't about to let her stay somewhere that clearly had inadequate hotel security.

"I can't let you pay—"

"Yes, you can. Besides, I'm manager, and it's our slow season. I'm sure we have a couple of rooms available." The lines around her eyes creased in worry. "It's complimentary," he added. "It won't come out of my pocket, either." He tilted his head back and forth. "And if you're that worried about it, you can ease your conscience by writing a review after your stay with us." He held out his hand. "Come on."

Her eyes twinkled as she looked up at him, and she accepted his hand. "You can't buy a good review from me, Matthew McGuire. I have my integrity."

The softness of her touch took him off guard. He let go the moment she had her balance. "If you're not one hundred percent satisfied, your room is compliment— Oh, wait…"

She laughed. "Point taken."

"Besides, you're going to love it." He couldn't help bragging over his hotel. The last two years, he'd worked hard to make it the premier destination for conference attendees, and the top brass had noticed. Which was how he'd been promoted so fast.

He glanced down at her dainty foot within her flat. It was red, most likely from the ice. "How is it?"

"Almost as good as new."

"Isabelle, what did the police say?"

"They didn't think the two incidents were connected." Her hand clasped her necklace again.

"Seems a bit coincidental, don't you think?"

"They figure I somehow showed I had cash."

"They assume the men with knives—"

She flinched at the word. "They say I've had an unfortunate experience with San Antonio crime."

Granted, he wasn't a woman walking the streets alone, but the statement didn't ring true to him. If she couldn't offer the police any reason why someone would be targeting her, then they would be grasping at straws. "And what do you think?"

"It seems a bit much to take on face value, but I can't offer another explanation for why this happened to me." Her face was lined with worry. She didn't seem to be holding anything back. She looked genuinely surprised.

She offered him a smile, but it didn't reach her eyes. "I'd better gather my things."

Ten minutes later, Matt sat in a cab with Isabelle. He'd called ahead, and his staff assured him they had a room ready for her. "We didn't have a king-size," Matt explained. "I hope a standard double room will be adequate."

She rolled her eyes. "Oh, well, I guess you get what you pay for. You'll have to wait to find out what I think until my review."

He stared at her, a warmth building in his chest. He had loved this girl, and she'd never known it.

The mischievous glint in her eyes dimmed. "Oh, no." She yanked out her phone. "I'm over an hour late to the networking dinner. It was supposed to start at seven."

"I'm sure they'll understand given the circumstances."

"That's not the point. I promised Hank I'd take every opportunity. He—we need this."

Was she in a relationship with this Hank? Nope, he wouldn't ask. Not his business. "Let's get you settled and get you to that dinner. Which restaurant?" he asked.

She told him as the cab pulled in front of his hotel.

He paid the driver and helped her out of the cab. "That's just across the street, under the bridge, on the left side of the River Walk. We can't get you any closer by taxi."

So much for showing off with a grand tour. He stared into the dark night. After the day she'd had, he couldn't let her go walking alone—with a weak ankle—through the throng of tourists and occasional muggers. "On second thought, I'll take you straight there myself."

She looked up at him. "You don't have to. You've done so much already."

Yes, there were still remnants of the stubborn girl he'd known. "Izzy, I'd like to escort you there. While I think you'll be safe in the tourist sections, ease my conscience by promising me someone will walk you back to the hotel when you're done."

She straightened. "Deal. But what about my luggage?"

Matt called for the bellhop, who instantly recognized him. "Yes, sir?"

"Please take Ms. Barrows's luggage and put it behind the front desk for me."

"Do you have a hotel safe?" Isabelle asked.

"Of course."

"Would it be okay if I put my laptop in it?" She pulled it out of her messenger bag and cried out at the sight of a bent corner. "I'd forgotten about this." She studied it for a moment. "It still should work. So, can I use your safe?"

Matt nodded slowly. "Yes. Frank can put it in the safe." Matt took the laptop from her and handed it to his employee. "Straight to the safe."

Frank nodded and took off with the rollaway and computer. Matt watched him to make sure he was making a beeline to the front-desk area. But he couldn't help but wonder if Isabelle was hiding something. Was her laptop the reason her room had been ransacked? And by agreeing to store it, was he putting a target on his own hotel?

Her eyes softened as she took his offered arm. "Thank you. You've gone above and beyond for someone you haven't seen in years."

As they made their way down the stone steps into the dimly lit cacophony, he hoped it would be enough to keep her safe.

THREE

She hated relying on Matt. This was not how she imagined experiencing the River Walk and the conference. In her mind, she was a strong, independent, single woman strolling confidently down the sidewalks. And little girls would look from the hands of their parents and wonder what glamorous job she had…

Okay, Isabelle was a dreamer and knew it. But still, this wasn't going as planned. They emerged from the curved stone staircase onto the open River Walk. Music from a mariachi band filtered through laughter and trees to her ears. Colorful patio umbrellas lined the right side. Tree branches hung over the river that sloshed precariously close to the sidewalks, likely from the heavy rains last week.

Ducks squawked. One hopped onto an empty chair of an outdoor diner. It was like a hidden world underneath the city. Isabelle flinched as a man brushed past her. She stepped closer to Matt.

"We're almost there," he said. They passed the colorful tables, and the music faded in the background as he led her inside the waiting area of a posh restaurant. "See your party?"

On her tiptoes, she spotted the graying head of Darren Allen, the CEO of Endangered Robotics. He leaned back in his seat to talk to another man. Their plates held the remains of their meals. A waiter approached their table and handed them each a black book. "Oh, no. They've already got their bills."

Isabelle was raised knowing that if you arrived five minutes early to an event, you were actually ten minutes late. Joining the party this tardy pained her. And to top it off, there wasn't an empty spot for her to sit, if even for a few minutes.

Matt looked over her shoulder. "At least they aren't completely done. Some of them are still eating. Look, there is an empty table right next to them. You can get a little networking in before they leave while you wait for some food." He leaned over and spoke to the hostess.

The thought of sitting alone at the small square table put a pit in her stomach. She'd look pathetic to the rest of the attendees. No, she'd be better off cutting her losses and trying again tomorrow. But the hostess was already waving at her. "Right this way."

Darren Allen caught her eye. Oh, great. If she turned around now, they would all know she was too chicken to eat alone. She gulped and looked over her shoulder. "Okay. Well, thanks, Matt."

He nodded and touched her elbow. "See you in a bit."

Darren waved at her. "There's the new golden girl we've been hearing all about. Your presentation must be something else to get added at the last minute. We were hoping you'd have joined us for dinner to tell us about it."

Every giant in the industry of oceanographic research and innovation looked up at her. "I'm sorry. I was held up."

A man about her age turned in his chair. His blue eyes twinkled up at her. "Oh, so you must be the expert of fluid dynamics I keep hearing about." He held out his hand. "Robert."

"Struther," she finished for him. "You were the youngest winner ever of the underwater robot competition before you were swept up as the lead researcher for Robotic Aquatic." She cringed inwardly. She sounded like a fangirl, which she was, but she needed him to see her more like a colleague.

He shrugged. "Vice president now, but yes.

I expect I'll never fully leave the lab." He gestured to her chair. "Please. Don't let us keep you from ordering. We're just wrapping up." He nodded at the rest of the group. She waved awkwardly at everyone, but most of them just nodded back.

Struther stood. "Nice to meet you…uh…"

"Isabelle Barrows." She shook his hand. "From Hayden Research Station."

He stepped closer and lowered his voice. "Any spoilers you can give about your presentation?"

The unexpected heat from his proximity made her want to squirm, but this was exactly the kind of connection she needed to make for the institute. "Um, I think it would be detrimental to rush that conversation. Perhaps another time?"

He stared into her eyes. "I look forward to it." He slipped a business card from his pocket and handed it to her, cupping her hand in both of his palms. "You have my number."

Darren stood and shook her hand. "I hope you're not eating all by your lonesome, sweetheart."

She flinched at the term of endearment. But she supposed a lot of older men spoke that way.

Matt appeared out of nowhere and pulled out the chair on the opposite side of the table.

"Sorry to keep you waiting, Izzy." He held out a hand to the CEO. "Matt McGuire."

Darren grinned. "Ah. Perfect place to enjoy young love." He winked at Isabelle. "Until tomorrow."

The group left, leaving Isabelle and Matt alone. "Where'd you come from?" she asked.

"Didn't think I'd let you eat alone, did you?" He flashed a sheepish grin. "I realized I was hungry, and you looked uneasy. Did I overstep? Is it okay if I join you?"

Relief coursed through her body. "Yes, please." She finally sat, keenly aware the men in the group were making their way out of the restaurant. Her pride wouldn't leave Matt's gesture alone, though. "I mean, I would've been fine, but...thank you."

Darren and Robert stopped at the entrance doors. Through the window, the lights from above highlighted what looked like a tense interchange. "I wonder what they're talking about."

"Who are they?" Matt's gaze remained on the menu.

"The older man runs a company I would've killed to work at fresh out of college. He leads Endangered Robotics. They use drones to keep poachers away from rare animals, but the cool thing is they're expanding to under-water operations."

Matt's eyes widened. "And the other?"

"His company just landed a defense con-tract worth thirty million dollars." She glanced over her shoulder. The interchange seemed to be done. "I shudder to think just how much he makes."

"I take it not as much as you."

Isabelle laughed aloud. "Please. You saw the hotel room my institute could afford. We're a bare-bones outfit. But I hope to change that by luring some investors with my research."

The waiter came and took their orders. Matt leaned on his elbows. "This is an oceanology conference, right? What could be worth mil-lions of dollars?"

"You've heard about dolphins being trained for the government? Well, that guy, for in-stance, invented an underwater autonomous vehicle that does the work of the dolphins, only better." For the briefest of moments it seemed the estranged years disappeared, and she was sharing everything with her best friend again.

Matt raised an eyebrow. "So, what about you? What are you working on?"

"Application of fish swarm behavior in an intelligent transportation system." The familiar pulse of electricity when she talked about her passion made her sit up taller and talk faster. "I've developed a new algorithm that takes in new factors of thermodynamics, fluid dynamics and currents in a way never done before with the potential of driving systems with bottleneck and obstacle avoidance."

Matt's mouth parted slightly. His eyes flickered. "Uh…I don't suppose you could repeat that in English?"

She deflated in her chair. "Drones. Think underwater drones."

His eyebrows rose. "Oh. Cool."

"My boss had to pull a lot of strings so I could present here. The goal is to network and share just enough of my research to get investors to partner with us." And if she failed, who knew how much longer the institute, and therefore her job, would even exist?

Sure, she felt confident another company would hire her, but it was the last thing she wanted. Finally having a permanent home meant something, and she would do whatever it took to hold on to it. Her coworkers had become like family to her—with the exception of Hank, who already was—and she wasn't about to give it up.

The waiter placed salads in front of them. Matt's forehead creased in concern. "Is that why you wanted your laptop in the safe? Do you think the hotel-room incident could have something to do with it?"

"It's probably silly to think someone would be after my research. My boss has taken every precaution to make sure no one even knows enough to want to steal it, but—"

"After the day you've had, you want to play it safe."

"Exactly."

They ate in awkward silence. He cleared his throat as the salads disappeared and the meals came. "Since I don't know if we'll have another chance to talk, I'd like to clear the air."

She fidgeted with her silverware. "It's not necessary. It's not like those things you said were lies."

"Izzy, I didn't mean—"

"No, really, Matt. I get the Bro Code and all that. You were looking out for Randy. Besides, the whole thing was stupid. At the time, I wasn't even interested in Randy."

His mouth dropped. "You weren't?"

"Nope." What was she doing? She needed to stop her mouth, but the adrenaline from the evening and the combined exhaustion made her mouth run on and on. "I actually liked you. And then my girlfriends convinced me to try that stunt to make you jealous. But you know what's the craziest of all? I ended up with Randy anyway. He said he never would've known who I was if it wasn't for you. Isn't that funny?"

Matt stared at her, his expression unreadable. "You what?"

"Randy and I ended up at the same college. He had a football scholarship."

Matt pursed his lips. "Huh." He coughed and rearranged the food on his plate.

"And he assured me the stuff you said about me didn't bother him. So, see? We can move on."

"Well, uh, that's, uh…a relief. Are you still—"

"No. Don't worry. My crush on you is gone." She put a hand on her chest. "No threat here."

He cleared his throat. "I was going to ask if you were still with Randy."

"Oh." Her face heated. "No. He got offered a job as a pharmaceutical rep. I just couldn't do that kind of life."

Matt's eyes softened. "The traveling?"

His question caught her off guard. She managed to nod. "A long-distance relationship and moving are off the table. I want to stay somewhere for the long haul."

Isabelle stared at her empty plate. She'd talked and eaten so fast, it didn't register what the food had tasted like. The reminder that Matt knew enough to understand her desire without clarification rankled her for some reason. So much so, she wasn't fast enough to pay for the check before he'd already taken care of it.

He escorted her to the door. A breeze wove through the River Walk. She shivered. The temperature must've dropped twenty-some degrees since the afternoon. In a heartbeat, Matt took off his suit jacket and handed it to her.

"For the walk back."

She accepted. The jacket did more than provide warmth. It somehow made her feel safer, as if wearing armor. She looked like someone's girlfriend. She hadn't been one of those for over a year now.

Her ankle hurt less as she joined the throng of tourists. The ice and rest had done the job. Matt had to step behind her, single file, as there wasn't enough room to walk alongside each other and still allow the traffic to flow from the opposite direction. The jumble of tourists merging onto the sidewalk separated them by a couple of people.

A hand snaked around her wrist and yanked her off the walkway and into the darkness. A glint of metal appeared at her waist. "Scream and you die." The man pulled her up an incline and pushed her into a shadowed area behind a tree.

* * *

Matt nearly fell into the water when someone shoved past him. A woman grabbed his shirt and helped him upright. His focus had been elsewhere…specifically, on the fact that Isabelle had ended up with Randy after all. The incident in high school had been an immature ploy to get his attention? How ironic that he had responded with his own ploy by trying to drum up bad things to say about her.

So she'd come clean, but why couldn't he? Why hadn't he interrupted Isabelle and admitted he had liked her? Why hadn't he told her he never meant those hurtful things? His lips had refused to cooperate. Pride had paralyzed him. Again.

He scanned the tourists ahead of him. He'd completely lost sight of her. He strained his neck in an effort to spot Isabelle. No sign. He called her name, but the music and talking and laughter from all the restaurants swallowed up his voice.

Something reflected a light. On Marriage Island—a tiny, unlit inlet that jutted into the San Antonio River—a couple stood in the shadows against the tree. He almost looked away, but the profile looked remarkably like Isabelle's. He saw the outline of the man wrench a bag from her torso.

Matt vaulted through the crowd. As he rounded the tree, the man pointed a gun at Isabelle. "Hey!" As the man turned to aim the gun at him, Matt grabbed the assailant's arm and twisted it until the weapon dropped from his hand. The man punched Matt in the gut with his other arm.

Pain vibrated down his legs from the impact.

The man pulled a knife from his pocket and stabbed it into Isabelle's torso. She cried out and crumpled. Matt pulled his fist back and slammed it into the assailant's jaw.

The man stumbled backward until he took off into a run, the messenger bag bouncing off his hip. He ran around the tree, pushed tourists aside and dashed up a flight of stairs to the upper level of stores.

"Stop him," Matt shouted, but over the noise, he doubted anyone heard him. The creep didn't even glance back before he slipped between two buildings and disappeared.

Isabelle's hands held her stomach. Matt dropped to his knees. He looked past the tree and yelled for help at a group passing by. He reached for Isabelle. How badly had she been stabbed?

She coughed. "He's getting away."

He couldn't call for an ambulance without his phone, which still resided in the inner pocket of his suit jacket. He reached for her and prepared himself for the worst as his eyes focused on the rip in his suit, where she'd been stabbed. He pulled back the jacket slowly, inwardly cringing at what he might find.

Instead of blood he saw only fabric. His eyes lifted to her face.

She pressed her hand on her stomach. "It didn't pierce me. The force of it just hurt. Your jacket… Was there something in the pocket?" Her frown cleared as she pulled out his phone and wallet. Cracks radiated across the screen. In the center of the phone he could see the point of impact. If the blade had hit flesh… He gulped.

Her right hand reached for his wrist.

"Isabelle, you could've been—"

"But I wasn't. You saved my life," she whispered. Her eyes filled. "He got away with everything. My phone, my wallet, my tablet… It's all gone."

He squeezed her hand. "All replaceable." Unlike her.

Two policemen ran up to the tree. One took a knee. "Ma'am, do you need an ambulance?"

Twenty minutes passed before the officers were finished with their questions. Matt half listened to their reassurances to Isabelle that if she came to the police station for the report, she would likely still be able to fly home without an ID.

One officer stepped away while he listened to his radio. He approached again. "Ma'am, you said you were pursued earlier today by two men? Was this attack made by one of the same men?"

"No." She frowned. "I'm positive."

"Were there any witnesses to the earlier event?"

She narrowed her eyes. "Just Matt."

The officer gave him a long glance. "And you were the only witness to this altercation, as well?"

Matt leaned back on his heels. Was the officer implying they were making the incidents up? "We were surrounded by witnesses. Surely someone saw something." He waved behind him to the sidewalk.

"If they did, they didn't stick around to tell their story." The other officer narrowed his eyes.

Matt threw his hands up in the air. "This can't be a coincidence."

The officer ignored him and addressed Isabelle. "I assure you it's very unusual for one of our tourists to be a victim of so much crime in one day, ma'am. Were you carrying anything valuable that would draw attention?"

Isabelle grabbed her sparkling necklace. The temptation to ask who gave her that welled up in Matt again. "Only the usual conference-attendee stuff," she said. "Wallet, tablet, phone—you know, basically my whole world." She smiled weakly.

Matt recalled the way she'd begged for him to put her laptop in the hotel safe. She had been carrying it in her messenger bag. What if the people who tore up her room were looking for the information that was on her laptop?

The memory of the man shoving the knife into Isabelle made him flinch. If he'd been after the laptop and thought he'd grabbed it, then why stab her? His blood ran cold. Did someone want her out of the picture?

The police officers repeated their safety advice to her and walked away.

Matt met her eyes. "Why didn't you tell them about the laptop?"

She looked uneasy. "It wasn't pertinent."

"Wasn't it?" He crossed his arms across his chest. "I think it's time you told me more about these underwater drones."

FOUR

The light emphasized Matt's dark eyes. How many times had she dragged out conversations with him just for an excuse to keep looking into his eyes? Her cheeks heated at the thought, and she moved her gaze to the cobblestone beneath her feet.

She wasn't a teenager anymore. She had better things to think of, more practical things. They'd changed. It was just the memory of a childhood crush. That was all. She'd get over it. She had to.

"Isabelle?" Matt repeated.

"Okay. Basically my life was thrown into chaos a couple weeks ago. I had a theory, and when I proved it, Hank used all his connections, and probably all his money, and got me a spot at the conference not only as an attendee but also as a presenter. It was very rushed."

"That algorithm you were trying to tell me about?"

"Yes. It's not the easiest thing to explain if I don't want to put you to sleep." She studied his expression so she'd have a baseline to reference if she started to lose him. "Nothing that's been applied, but there's the potential."

"Of underwater drones?"

"Not exactly." She waved at the river next to them as they walked closer to the stairs that would lead them back to the city streets. "Imagine there was a way to track fish and currents. That it could also be so undetectable that it wouldn't disturb wildlife. To do that, we'd need the research to enable the drones to mimic the wildlife, right? Swarms of these drones could be for tracking and reconnaissance, not so much for attacking…although I admit, there could be the potential."

His brow furrowed.

She tried again. "Okay. How about this? Imagine something that could even change currents if you needed it to. Wouldn't the US Navy find that useful?"

His eyes widened. "Your research could do that?"

She shrugged. "Technology has missed some vital pieces to make it work. Namely the research."

"And you've got the missing pieces."

"I have at least one piece, but I believe it will lead me to the other pieces."

"With the funding you're trying to get this week." He offered his arm as they ascended the stairs, and she took it. Matt kept looking over his shoulder. She knew he wanted to stay alert and keep her safe, but the constant checking unnerved her. "I'm still upset at the cops' insinuation this was random crime," he said. "The ransacked room combined with the attack is too much."

"I know." She really hoped he would stop talking about it so her heart rate could return to normal. "But from the police's point of view, it's been different people. I don't even know if my research is connected with it."

They crossed the street to the hotel entrance. He jolted to a stop at the automatic doors. His eyes widened. "What if someone *wants* it to look like random crimes?"

Her gut twisted. She could accept that if the man hadn't tried to stab her. The thought that someone wanted to kill her... Well, her mind wouldn't let her dwell on that possibility. "We're jumping to conclusions that I don't want to explore, Matt." Or she'd never be able to sleep.

"You're right. I'm sorry. Listen, I'll do whatever I can to help keep you safe."

She looked down at her empty hands. All her personal information was on her tablet and phone, as if her life was spread open for that knife-wielding stranger to see. Assuming he could get past her passwords.

Matt had already done more than she could've asked, but right now she needed to contact the credit-card companies and, more important, her boss. "Do you guys have a business computer I can use here?"

He raised an eyebrow. "You can use your laptop. I'll get it out of the safe."

"No, I can't. It doesn't have a network card. Zero wireless capabilities. For security reasons."

He folded his arms across his chest. "Security?"

"It's becoming more common for researchers like me. About a year ago, another research center—a contractor for the defense department—had their data hacked. The sensitive information wasn't stolen because the equipment they used for that purpose had no online capabilities. Hank took that as a lesson and made sure any of my data was compiled and analyzed only on a laptop without network cards."

"I never would've thought ocean research was that valuable." Matt whistled. "Well, speaking of hacking, I wouldn't use our pub-

lic computers to check on your credit cards.
And while I can make your room complimentary, I can't waive long-distance charges. My
place is nearby. You can use my computer and
phone. I insist. Stay here, and I'll get your laptop from the safe."

Being in debt to a guy she used to have a
crush on was not on her agenda for the week.
She already owed him for the room. More important, she owed him her life. But when she
thought of it that way, using his computer didn't
seem like so much extra.

He approached with the laptop in his hands.
"I've got it. Follow me." He turned to walk
down a hallway.

She looked around the marbled lobby at the
plush couches and sparkling chandeliers. The
immense difference in hotels struck her. Cheerful walls the color of lemon cheesecake complemented the navy runner. The only smells
came from the coffee shop in the back of the
lobby. The thought of enjoying a latte in the
morning served as a balm to her—

Her stomach sank. Her wallet was in the
hands of that goon. This wasn't the type of
place that came with complimentary breakfast.
The conference came with very few meals, and
it was only Monday night. Aside from the prepaid awards dinner on Tuesday and a boxed

dinner on Wednesday, she was on her own for food. She didn't have a way to pay for anything.

Her fingers moved to grip her messenger bag but met air. She had nothing. The severity of the situation hit her all at once, as if walls were closing in on her. A shuffle behind her pushed her forward. She wanted nothing more than to be alone. Being among strangers never used to bother her, but a new vulnerability she'd never experienced before made her legs twitch, ready to run.

Matt turned and made eye contact with someone behind them. "Can I help you?"

She looked over her shoulder. The man, dressed in a black short-sleeve polo, tan pants and a baseball hat, spun on his heel with a wave. He walked away.

"That was weird." Matt watched the back of the man until he was no longer in sight.

"Really? It seems to have become the norm." And she didn't know what to make of it.

"Maybe he forgot something."

She nodded. She wasn't sure, but he kind of looked like the man who had been across the street from the hotel, watching her with a newspaper in his hands, sans his jacket from before.

Matt's eyes locked on hers. His concerned gaze drew her a step closer, and she realized how desperate she was to be comforted. The man could give the best hugs, if memory served her right. She blinked. What was she doing? She took a step back.

He straightened. "We're here." He took out a real key, not a card, and unlocked a door with an embossed plate that read Director of Operations.

The door swung open to a gorgeous suite, or in this case, apartment. Gray tile floor instead of carpet reflected the light from the chandelier. Past the entryway, an Oriental rug complemented the silver couches with teal cushions. She spun around, taking it in. A kitchenette peeked behind a half wall, and an open door to the left revealed a king-size bedroom complete with sheer curtains surrounding it, almost like a canopy. "Are all the rooms like this?" She tried to keep the eager grin off her face. This was luxury.

"Not to this extent or size, but similar." He pulled his own laptop out of the cherry desk and entered his username and password. "I'll give you privacy to make your calls and check your accounts."

He walked behind the kitchenette wall, and she almost called him back—which was ridiculous. She could handle being alone. She dropped into the leather desk chair. After she pulled up each credit-card company and froze the cards, she dialed Hank's number.

"Isabelle," he exclaimed before she could say a word. "I've been trying to reach you for the past hour."

"You have?" She leaned onto her elbow and rested her tightening forehead against her palm.

"Yes. We were hacked today. I wanted you to know before the conference gossip got to you. I've already assured the conference organizers that it will in no way affect your presentation."

"Hank, listen—"

"I told them the research is uncompromised, and you're the only one with access to it. That seemed to appease the board members. They've had so much interest in your topic, they've bumped you to a bigger venue. You'll be the keynote for Friday morning."

Isabelle blinked a couple of times, trying to process. That was huge. "Someone is after the research."

"I know, but I'm telling you, they didn't get it."

"Hank, I mean here. Men have been after me." She relayed the events of the past few hours. Hank remained quiet, but she could hear his breathing grow ragged. "It's okay, Hank. They haven't succeeded."

"I've dipped into my retirement." Hank's

voice shook softly. "I can't send you money. I'm tapped out. I should've never sent you there. I don't know what made me think I could do this."

Isabelle's heart squeezed. She was the reason. He'd hired her to work straight out of college. She'd talked him into upgrading his technology and insisted she could put the small institute on the map. And he'd believed in her. If the institute failed, it would be her fault.

"Come home, Isabelle. We need to keep you safe." He cleared his throat. "I'll figure something else out."

"No, Hank. I'm fine. Don't worry." She fingered the diamond heart hanging from her neck. Her chest heated at the thought of letting him down. She'd had no idea he'd taken personal financial risk. He'd seen the potential in her. She couldn't let it be for nothing. "The cops think it's likely random crime. I'm in good hands. I promise."

The words were technically true, even if she didn't believe them herself. Hank had inherited the private research center several years ago. While he didn't have the academic background to research himself, he had a love for all things ocean. He shared that passion with the community by offering a donation-only aquarium and tide-pool tours. She'd almost refused his offer to hire her since he also was her uncle. But having family in the place she settled down was so appealing.

When he'd hired her, he'd bent over backward to help Isabelle in any way he could to pursue any hypothesis she wanted. The way he'd believed in her endeared Hank to her like a second father.

"Oh. Random crime? Good," Hank said. "I mean, crime is not good, but that makes me feel better. Are you sure you're okay? You have enough money to last the week?"

"I'll be fine." Somehow she would be, even if that meant living on the remaining granola bars and gummy bears in her suitcase. "Good night, Hank," she said tenderly. She hung up and lifted her gaze.

Matt stood at the kitchen entrance, holding two mugs, his face ashen.

She was taken. Figured. Why it bothered him so much, he couldn't pinpoint. But the love on her face was undeniable. He wouldn't ask about this Hank guy, though. He had no right and no reason. Isabelle was just a friend and would remain such. She'd be out of his life once again in a week.

He cleared his throat. "I made you some hot

chocolate." He set the mugs on coasters on the coffee table in front of the couch.

Her eyes lit up. "Sounds perfect." She sat down on the cushion next to him.

"You can take it to the desk if you have more calls."

"No, I think I'm okay for now. Thank you." Her face transformed at the sight of the mug. "Whipped cream and…" She tilted her head. "Cinnamon stick?"

He nodded. "It's a recipe one of our restaurant chefs passed on. You make the cocoa from a dark chocolate bar with cinnamon and sugar to taste."

"Oh? You have close *friends* within the hotel?"

The way she said *friends* made him smile. Was she trying to sniff out if he had a girl-friend? "Yes, I suppose. But I don't blur the employer-employee relationship."

Her eyebrows furrowed. "No, of course not. I wasn't implying—" She leaned forward to pick up the mug.

"But I don't judge people who do." He shook his head slightly. Why did that have to slip out?

Her hands froze in midair. She regarded him with a curious look on her face. "I guess it's different for me. The institute has practically turned into a family business." She pulled the mug up to her lips and took a tentative sip. "Oh, Matt, this is delicious." She leaned back into the cushion.

"Family as in future husband, then?" He clamped his jaw shut. Why couldn't he let this go?

She laughed, and a puff of whipped cream floated to the coffee table. "Sorry." She leaned forward and used a napkin to wipe it up. "No. Hank is my uncle. I'd do anything for him. I try to separate the family from the business, so I don't call him *uncle*, but he's made the place feel like home." She twisted to look at him directly. "You know, I've always dreamed of getting to settle down in one place without having to move."

Matt did know. When asked what she wanted to be when she grew up, the answer would always be, *"I don't care as long as I don't have to move."* Apparently she found the career to match her brilliance, and he couldn't help but be happy for her.

She took another long sip. "Hank even invited me to spend Christmas with his extended family. It's been so nice." Whipped cream lined the top of her lips. He reached over and brushed it off gently with his thumb. He yanked his arm back at the realization of what he'd done.

Her eyes widened and her lips parted, but she said nothing.

"Sorry." He tried to form a joke about good customer service but decided it was best to move on. He bent forward and grabbed one of the napkins. "Here you go."

She blotted her lips with it. "I guess when you've spent as much time as we have together…"

She never finished her sentence. Matt really wanted to know the rest of her thought, but he didn't want to focus anymore on his faux pas. He took his own drink of the cocoa, taking care to make sure the whipped cream didn't leave a mark on him. "Let's talk about tomorrow." He needed to change the subject before the heat in his chest made its way to his cheeks. "Can you access the conference schedule online?"

"Yes. Why?"

"Let's figure out where you might be vulnerable. To avoid moments like today."

"You've done enough, and—"

"Isabelle, humor me."

Her blue eyes hit him. The intensity in her gaze disarmed him, and he felt sure for half a second that she could see his very thoughts. She smiled, and he fought the urge to ask her a million questions about their years apart, to experience the same connection they'd once shared. Isabelle stood and brought over the laptop, typed an address into the browser and pointed at the screen.

Their shoulders touched as she settled back into the couch cushions. The ends of her hair brushed against him, and he remembered how she used to lean her head on his shoulder and tell him all about her day at school.

This Isabelle sat rigid, though. "So, as you can see, I'll be inside the conference center for the entirety of the day."

"Except for lunch."

"Well, yes, but I wasn't planning to leave the building."

Matt pictured the conference area in his mind's eye. Attendees would likely flock to Rosario's or the Amaya Deli, but Isabelle had no wallet, so she wouldn't be joining them. If he offered room service for breakfast and a sack lunch from the restaurant for lunch, he felt sure Isabelle would refuse. But he couldn't let her starve. Matt made a mental note of what time the conference started to ensure his staff would deliver both before she left.

Transportation was another problem. Taxis were expensive. While he could afford a few out of his personal funds, he kept to a tight budget so he could pay off his student loans faster. But what he didn't have in cash, he could access through his network of connections. Both times, Isabelle was attacked on foot. So if she had the advantage of wheels, maybe that would be enough, especially if he knew the drivers. He'd start making phone calls as soon as he said good-night.

"So, aside from the employer-employee relationship, do you have friends here?"

Her question pulled him out of his thoughts like a slap. "What? Friends? Yeah...I guess. Sure."

Isabelle raised an eyebrow. "You don't sound so sure."

He pointed to the computer. "Deep in thought is all." He sighed. "I talk to plenty of people each day."

"That's not what I asked." She slumped a bit until her head rested on the top of the back of the couch, and she stared at the ceiling. "The Matt I used to know had tons of acquaintances but very few gut-level friends."

"True. I still talk to a couple of the guys back home. That's enough for me." He didn't want to admit that it got lonely at times. As long as he stayed busy, it didn't bother him until the hotel began running so smoothly he had no excuse not to take off a few evenings each week. He wasn't unhappy, but he did wish he had someone close enough to want more than "I'm good" as an answer to how he was doing.

"What about you?" he asked. "I seem to remember the same could be said about you."

"I was hoping you'd forgotten that." She winked. "It was easier back when I had the four crazy McGuire brothers as neighbors to entertain me and pull me into their crazy antics. No excuses, though. I'm working at building friendships. I keep reminding myself that I don't have to move—" Her voice cracked ever so slightly. She straightened and blinked rapidly. "As long as I have a job, I get to stay put, you know? So I'm trying hard. I'm trying to make roots and push myself to make deeper connections with people. I get along great with my coworkers and the volunteers."

In other words, she was just like him. "No one else?"

She rolled her eyes. "You weren't supposed to turn my line of questioning on me. I'm trying. I just joined the women's Bible study at church."

He nodded. The first thing he'd done after getting settled was join the men's study at the closest church. Maybe she was better at lowering her walls than he was.

She squeezed her eyes closed and released a yawn.

That was his cue to call it a night. "Let me walk you to your room." His eyes caught something on the screen he hadn't noticed before. "What's this dinner thing tomorrow?"

She leaned forward. "Oh. An awards dinner for all attendees, which means another great chance for me to find some potential investors."

"At the Tower of the Americas? You'll need someone to walk you to the entrance. A taxi can get you close but not right up to the door."

"You've gone up the tower?"

"I've been meaning to, but haven't had a reason to go in yet."

She bit her lip and gave him a sidelong glance. "We could solve both our problems with my plus-one ticket."

He laughed. "Smooth, Izzy."

A lovely shade of mauve bloomed over her face. He used to be able to make her blush often. He'd forgotten how much he loved that.

"You don't have to," she said quickly.

"No take-backs. I'm already planning on it." He grinned. "Let's get you up to your room. I can't have my future reviewer not getting enough sleep. She might think it was the fault of the hotel."

They walked in silence to the front desk to retrieve her rolling suitcase. He enjoyed watching the reactions play on her face as she took in the ornate chandeliers all the way to the elevator. Not that he was responsible for the beauty of the hotel, but he was proud to work there. It wasn't his dream, but it was a satisfying job.

When they reached the sixth floor, he insisted on checking the room himself.

Isabelle whistled at the room. "Nice digs, Matt."

"Okay, there is a personal safe in each hotel room. It's big enough for your laptop. It even has an outlet so you can keep it charged. You can pick your own code to lock it, but feel free to bring it down to the front desk if you'd like. When I leave, use the dead bolt and the bar. Stick the door wedge underneath for additional safety."

Her forehead creased slightly as she nodded. "Thank you. For everything."

He racked his brain for anything else that might be useful. "If anyone knocks, even if it looks like a hotel employee, call me." He grabbed the hotel notepad and jotted down his direct line. As long as she was without a working cell phone, they would have to rely on the direct lines. In the morning, he'd see about a replacement. "Don't open the door for anyone."

Her eyes widened, and his attempt at reassuring her seemed to have had the opposite effect.

"You can rest easily now." He placed a hand on her shoulder. "You're safe here."

As he left her room, he prayed he had told her the truth.

FIVE

Isabelle stared out the window of the catering van. Her head pounded with the stress and busyness the day had brought, especially after a sleepless night. She had flinched at every sound inside and outside the hotel's walls.

The morning had started with Matt knocking at her door. He'd brought her breakfast, coffee and a gourmet sack lunch to take with her. And to top it off, he'd arranged for his linen supplier to drop her off at the conference free of charge and a local caterer to return her.

She could see him now, standing next to the valet at the hotel driveway, waiting for her arrival. He beamed at the sight of her, and Isabelle wasn't sure how to process all the emotions hitting her at once. She'd forgotten what it was like to have someone so thoughtful in her life, someone who smiled at her very presence. And yet she needed to push down the all-too-familiar attraction. He'd always seen her as a friend and nothing more. That had to be at the front of her mind.

Besides, even if there were mutual attraction, it wouldn't work. She had what she'd always wanted in Oregon, a permanent home. There was no future for them besides rekindled friendship, which would be more than enough. It had to be.

Matt waved his thanks at the caterer and led her inside. He wore a classic-fit suit in a shade of blue so light, it was almost silver, and it emphasized his wide shoulders and the brass highlights in his hair and eyes. "How was your day?"

"Filled with countless workshops and lectures." Without her tablet, she found it hard to keep up with note taking. She'd left her laptop in the room's safe and planned to keep it there until her presentation at the end of the week. So for now, she used hotel pens and notepads to fill in the gap. "Thanks again for making it so easy to get to and from the conference. I'll just be a minute and then I'll be ready for the awards dinner."

She hustled to her room and changed into a power suit, a red jacket with gold accents and black pants. In five minutes flat, she was back in the lobby. Except, Matt was engaged in a conversation with someone. It was the same man who seemed to have been following them in the hall the night before. She took a step closer and stiffened.

Matt stood with his arms crossed over his chest. "Well, Mr. Frazer. Let me know if you have any questions."

The man looked over Matt's shoulder at her. Isabelle glanced away so she didn't appear to be eavesdropping. She spotted the security guard near the front door, and it helped calm her heart.

"I will," the man replied. "I just like to get the feel of a place before I get serious about booking. Doing it in all the other locations, as well. Don't look now, but it seems like an attractive lady is hoping to get your attention."

Her cheeks heated. Apparently she wasn't as nonchalant as she thought.

Matt glanced at her and did a double take. It wasn't lost on Isabelle that he seemed to appreciate the change in her outfit. He smiled. "Yes, well, I get to escort her to dinner tonight."

"Ah, young love," Frazer replied.

Isabelle hated being talked about as if she weren't there. And now the man's assumptions could embarrass Matt. "It's business," she interjected.

Matt frowned and turned back to Frazer. Was he irritated she'd joined the conversation?

He pulled out a business card. "Take your time looking around. Enjoy a free coffee on me." He turned around, and they fell in step toward the glass doors.

"So, he wasn't following us last night?"

"I honestly don't think so," he said. "It's not unusual for people to want to see if our accommodations and service are as good as we promise on the websites. He's checking out the hotel for a possible future event. If he gets serious, I'll give him the tour." He waved to the driveway. "Shall we?"

A taxi waited underneath the awning. "I don't have any mo—"

"My treat," he answered. "Like you said, I've never been to the Tower before."

It might've been her imagination, but it seemed Matt paled a bit. The driver wove rapidly within traffic, and they sat in silence for the five-minute ride. At the parking lot drop-off, Matt placed a hand on her back and looked around wildly while keeping an almost impossible pace to the Tower doors.

Once inside, she recognized other conference attendees waiting in line for the elevator. A man wearing a white polo shirt waved them in and welcomed them to the Tower. Her introvert tendencies kept her from engaging with the attendees outside the actual workshops, which was counterproductive to finding investors.

She took a step closer to Matt as the doors closed. Her stomach flipped as the elevator shot upward. Almost instantly the glass walls revealed a beautiful view of San Antonio. As the recorded voice piped in interesting facts about the building, she marveled at the sight. Matt's rigid form didn't move an inch. His gaze remained on the button panel.

She bit her lip. She'd forgotten he was terrified of heights. Whenever he'd worked with his dad in construction, he'd kept both boots firmly on the ground. It was why he'd never followed in his dad's footsteps. No wonder he'd hadn't visited the Tower before now. But why did he agree to go with her? Just to keep her safe? Her heart swelled, but she didn't want to embarrass him in a box full of people.

She needed to keep his mind off it. She stepped closer to him. "So, tell me—what's the hardest part of your job?"

His shoulders relaxed slightly, but his gaze never wavered. "Making sure conference attendees can live in harmony," he answered quietly. Just above a whisper. "The year I started working there, both the Texas Democratic Party and the Young Republicans were scheduled to hold meetings at the hotel in the same week.

So now I watch out for a bad match. Wouldn't want a jewelry convention at the same time as a kleptomaniac convention."

She laughed but noticed his face was pale. "Funny." She put a hand on his shoulder, hoping to ground him. The heat radiating from his strong arms took her off guard, though, and her own knees felt a little weak.

"So when someone wants to book with us, I try to make sure it's the best fit. For instance, that man, Mr. Frazer, didn't want to tell me yet what kind of event he's thinking of booking. Not unusual when someone doesn't want a sales pitch, but on the other hand, I won't even take him seriously until I know." He shrugged. "It's actually kind of odd. We're the premier conference location in the city." He flushed and gave her a side grin. "Didn't mean to brag. But most people do try to win me over instead of the other way around. We get booked up far in advance."

He spoke faster than usual, and some color was returning to his face.

"The event room will be to your right," the elevator operator said.

The doors opened, and Matt practically shot out of the confined space. Poor guy. He made a beeline for the spread of hors d'oeuvres but skipped the food and instead took a giant cup of lemonade and gulped it down. "Hot in here, isn't it?" He loosened his necktie a bit and smiled. "Much better."

Sandra Parveen, the organizing committee chair, grabbed her arm. Her hair looked stiff, likely from too much hair spray. Though it probably looked better than Isabelle's frizzing waves.

"Oh, Isabelle," Sandra said. "Hank called me last night. Are you okay?"

She looked to Matt and tried to process what Sandra could be talking about. Had Hank called Sandra to inform her about all the attempts to steal the research?

"Getting hacked," Sandra said, this time softer. The fear of hacking was a very real threat in the world of research. Just a month prior, West Coast Ocean Institute was hacked and their proprietary research made public.

Isabelle forced a smile. "Didn't Hank tell you my swarm research wasn't touched?"

"Oh, yes, but it has to make you nervous. You know we have Blake, an IT guy on the conference organizing committee, here, as well. If you need any extra security measures, I'm sure he'd be glad to help. Do you want me to call him over?"

"Thank you. I feel confident it's secure right now, but I'll keep it in mind."

"Sure thing. There's been a lot of buzz about your little swarm theory research." She held up her fist and gave it a shake. "Can't disappoint the people."

"Miss Barrows." A deep Southern voice behind her prompted her to turn around. Darren Allen stood behind her. He'd changed into a white crisp shirt, a suit jacket and a turquoise bolo tie. "Darling," he drawled. "I've heard that you've had a bad experience with our fair city."

Isabelle felt her eyebrows rise. How would he know? She glanced over her shoulder to see if Matt was listening, but Sandra had accosted him and was peppering him with questions. "Where did you hear that?"

Darren whirled his hand around in the air. "Somebody here saw you with the police last night at the River Walk. If I had known you would be walking unaccompanied, I would've offered myself, hon."

The use of the endearments was beginning to grate on her nerves. "I wasn't unaccompanied. I'm fine."

He stepped so close she could smell some sort of strong cocktail on his breath. "You're in the big leagues now, kiddo. Some friendly advice—don't trust anyone." He lifted his chin so he looked down his nose at her. "The buzz is you've got some research that could prove to be very lucrative." He patted his chest. "Keep it close."

"You're not giving him insider information, are you?" Robert Struther stepped into their little circle. "I thought you promised me dibs."

It could've been her imagination, but she thought she saw Darren's eyes flash with anger. He straightened to his full height and nodded. "Think I'll get myself some appetizers. Remember what I said now, Miss Barrows." He winked and walked away.

Robert rolled his eyes. "If there were an award for least likely to be at an oceanology conference…"

"I know, right? But I don't fault him for wanting to expand," Isabelle gushed a little. To be treated like a peer by the famous Robert Struther was almost enough to send her giggling. She cleared her throat. "I'll be excited to see what Endangered Robotics does in pursuit of the ocean's health."

He shrugged. "Listen, I wasn't kidding earlier. Would you like to talk shop? How about right after this shindig?"

Robotic Aquatic would be the perfect company to fund their endeavors, and while Struther had been promoted to VP, he had been a lead researcher until recently. If anyone could see the potential in what she had to offer, he would. And the opportunity had practically fallen in her lap.

"Um, yes." She waved a hand at Matt behind her, who looked almost as pale as he had on the elevator. Sandra didn't seem to want to move on from talking to him. "I just need to check with my—" she didn't want to call him a "date" "—friend."

"I don't mind if he comes with. We won't take long. If I'm interested, we'll arrange a follow-up meeting. How about we meet at Cartographers after this? It's the revolving restaurant up a few more floors. We can talk over a cup of coffee." He looked over her head. "I imagine it'll be considerably more quiet there."

She nodded, and Struther walked away before they could settle on a time. She turned to hear Matt.

"Yes, well, I'd be glad to give you a tour to consider our facilities for your next conference."

"You do that." Sandra winked at Matt and smiled at Isabelle. "Excuse me. I need to make sure the caterers will serve dinner on time."

Matt exhaled as she walked away. "That was odd."

"What's sad is she's probably the most normal person in this room, aside from you."

He laughed aloud. "How's that?"

"I think her background is in public relations. The rest of us are obsessed with all things ocean and science."

Matt handed her a fresh glass of lemonade. "Speaking of everyone else, it might be a good idea to start asking yourself who could benefit from stealing your research."

Her throat tightened at his omission. They weren't *just* trying to steal her research. Thus far they seemed prepared to hurt…or kill her, as well. She really didn't want the reminder on such an important night. "It's hard to say. I can see multiple possible applications to my findings. The things that excite me most would be used for nonprofit." She worried her lip. "I don't want to be so prideful to assume it'll be the next big thing in defense, but if it fell in the wrong hands, there is a possibility it could compromise some of the work the US Navy is doing. In the right hands, it could replace older methods of surveillance."

"Didn't you say some of these companies here have multimillion-dollar contracts with the government performing those older methods?"

"Yes, but I'm inviting them to invest in the research from the ground up. If it turns out it's valuable, they would make a huge profit. So, I don't think that would make me a threat." As she said it, she questioned her logic. Would the companies see it that way? Or would her research make something more profitable obsolete?

Even as the thought formed, she remembered all the times she'd seen the water's smooth surface conceal turmoil and undertow below. Maybe the companies at the conference were hiding something. Was the plan to get investors naive?

"Isabelle? What is it?"

"Nothing." The ability to think out of the box proved helpful in research but gave her anxiety in other areas of life. Bottom line: it was pointless to worry about it when her research was nothing but an algorithm.

She told Matt about the upcoming meeting with Robert Struther.

"I'm glad he invited me along." He looked into her eyes. "Given the attacks, you have no way to know if he's trustworthy. I wouldn't want you to meet with him alone."

Despite the air-conditioning, warmth flooded her cheeks. Did he say that because he was worried about her or because he was jealous of Robert Struther? Scarier still, she didn't know which scenario pleased her more.

Matt did his best to smile and stay awake throughout the almost two hours of announcements, news, awards and talking points. The white folding chair creaked at his every move. He would definitely need that coffee Isabelle mentioned for her appointment with Struther.

And Matt wanted to be alert, as well. While Isabelle seemed to be of the notion that everyone in the conference was in the same boat as she was, he didn't buy it. She was an out-of-the-box thinker who didn't see herself for what she really was—a genius.

Sandra Parveen stepped up to the podium and dismissed them for the evening. He stood up fast, quickly taking in the view from the wall-to-wall windows on the other side of the room. He averted his gaze, though it was easier looking through them from this vantage point. It didn't feel like he was staring straight down, like he did from the elevator. And for some reason it was easier at night, maybe because he couldn't correctly gauge the distance from here to the sidewalks and streets below.

Unlike him, Isabelle seemed anything but bored. Her face flushed with excitement. Once she reached her goal of getting funding for the research project, would that mean the danger would stop? He assumed she'd have to share the research with the investor, and at that point it'd be less valuable to whoever was trying to steal it. At least, that was his hope.

He glanced at his watch. "When's your meeting?"

"I think now."

Matt matched her stride as she walked up to Struther, who was in midsentence with Darren Allen. The older man made his skin crawl. Maybe the sweet-talking Darren had good intentions—he did run a nonprofit, after all—but he made Matt feel like he was a crooked car salesman trying to sell Isabelle a junky car.

Struther turned to her before they'd reached him. "Isabelle," he said. "I'll be right behind you. Go ahead and get us a table, will you?" He didn't wait for Isabelle to answer before he was arguing about what sounded like a math equation with Darren.

Isabelle nodded and offered Matt a smile. "You still up for this? We have to get back in the elevator and go higher."

So she'd noticed his fear. And he'd thought he'd been so smooth in covering it up.

"The construction days," Isabelle offered, as if she could read his thoughts. "I assumed it was still an issue, which makes the fact that you came with me all the more special. Although you seem to have managed well."

She remembered. The back of his neck tingled with an odd, unsettling feeling. They'd been apart for years and yet she still knew his innermost wounds and secrets. The last summer before she'd moved, Dad had hired her to work for him as a secretary of sorts. She basically followed Dad around with a clipboard. She'd looked cute in a hard hat. But that wasn't what he recalled most.

It was the look on her face when he'd decided to ignore his well-developed fear of heights, mainly because Isabelle was there. Usually he would've made sure to get a ground-level job. Instead he offered to work up high, and Isabelle had witnessed the paralysis grab him. His brothers and one of the foremen had to pull him off the beam. It was the most humiliating experience of his life, followed by the realization that he couldn't follow the path his dad had set in front of him. He'd never be able to take over the family business.

"Don't worry about me." Matt placed a hand between Isabelle's shoulders and led her gently to the elevator. "The only thing I need is some coffee to wake up."

She laughed. There were two elevators and two operators. One already looked full. "Will we be able to go up to Cartographers?" she asked.

Just before the door closed, the operator with

the full elevator shook his head no. "We're only going down tonight, ma'am."

"Not true," the other man said after the other elevator's doors closed. "I will take you up."

"Are you sure?" Isabelle asked. "We're not the only ones that need to go up. I want to make sure he can." She pointed over her shoulder at Struther, who was still engaged in conversation behind them.

"It's not a problem." He ushered them in but waved the others back without explanation.

Matt shrugged apologetically at the crowd. "Maybe that means they're done taking orders for the night."

"It will be open for you," the operator answered.

The way he phrased it was odd. Isabelle didn't seem to think anything of it by the smile on her face. She turned to face the view while Matt maintained his stare at the elevator operator. The guy hadn't even tucked in his white polo. Wait. Was there a lump near the back of his waistband?

The man turned sideways as the elevator opened to a sign that read Cartographers Restaurant.

"Thank you," Isabelle said. She stepped out into the lobby area ahead of Matt. He rushed to join her.

As they rounded the corner to the bar area, they were met with a freestanding sign.

"Closed."

His spine straightened. The elevator operator should've known it was closed, unless…

Matt spun around to find him with a sick grin on his face.

"I guess I'll be your host for the evening," he said. He pointed a gun at Isabelle. "Party of two?"

Matt stepped in front of Isabelle and spread his arms wide as he pressed her backward. "Put the gun down. I'm sure we can come to an agreement without you needing that." He kept taking steps back, trying to move Isabelle as far away from the gunman as possible.

Her hands gripped the back of his suit jacket. She gasped. "It was a trap." Her forehead brushed against the center of his back. She whispered prayers underneath her ragged gasps for breath. "…please, Lord, please."

The operator's expression remained impassive. He didn't flinch or try to warn them as they backed away, which worried Matt even more.

Matt's heel brushed against a bar stool, and he realized he'd pressed Isabelle in between two stools and the bar counter. The farther away he got them from the gun, the better he felt, but unless they could run across the room to the restaurant portion, they were at the end of the line.

"Where is the research?" the man asked.

Matt narrowed his eyes. "You want the laptop? She doesn't have it."

The operator smirked. "Turns out I have time. Where is it?"

Isabelle peeked her head over Matt's shoulder. "Hotel safe."

Matt breathed a little easier. If the operator tried to lead them to the hotel to get the laptop, they would be on Matt's turf. Surely he'd be able to get them to safety and outwit the guy. And Isabelle hadn't specified that she'd left the laptop in her room safe, not the general hotel safe.

The man pulled a phone from his pocket. With his left hand, he pressed a button and spoke. "The hotel. Yes." The operator narrowed his eyes at Matt. "Behind the reservation counter?"

"Security office," Matt said. It wasn't true, but he hoped the Lord would forgive him for the misdirection.

"Yeah, I think we'll check the reservation counter first, thanks." The operator rolled his eyes and spoke back into the phone. "Call me back when you have it. Yeah, I'll wait."

"You'll let us go, then?" Isabelle asked.

The man looked over their heads. "Yeah, I'll let you go." The nonchalant way he said it and the manner in which the man squeezed his gun tighter told Matt the only place they'd be going was to their graves.

SIX

Isabelle's heart pounded so hard she was sure Matt could feel it. His body shielded most of her, but she could still read the gunman's body language. They wouldn't be leaving this room alive. Maybe she could throw him off his game. What would her dad do? The answer came immediately. Diversion tactics.

"Aren't you worried someone will show up on the elevator behind you?" she asked.

The man's gaze remained on her. He pulled out a set of keys and shook it. "Don't worry about that, darling. My elevator isn't going anywhere."

So even if they managed to get past him, they wouldn't be able to utilize the elevator. And the other operator had made it clear he was only taking people down. But maybe if the attendees got curious about where the other elevator operator was going, they would call someone...

The man followed her gaze and smirked.

"The other elevator isn't even scheduled to be operating tonight. So you might as well make yourself comfortable."

She felt the muscles in Matt's back tighten up at the cocky manner of the gunman. If she ever got her hands on Struther... Why would he set her up, though? His company had plenty of funds. Was he really that greedy? It wasn't as if she had a prototype ready to unleash in the seas. It was research. Could it really be that valuable?

Isabelle acted as if she were trying to get situated on one of the stools. Since Matt was in front of her, she hoped the man couldn't see she was actually peeking at what was on the counter behind her. Nothing.

Past the countertop was another story. A quick glance gave her a rough inventory: a metal drink shaker, bowls, long spoons, knives, a napkin holder and a couple of soda guns. If she stretched, she could reach any of it. But the man was too far away for it to do any good.

Besides, he had a gun. In a spoon versus gun battle, a gun always won.

But what if she could get him to come closer? He was the one who said they might as well relax while they waited for his partner to get her laptop. If she could get him to drop his guard, that might give them the edge. There was only one way she could think of to relax him. Bore him to death.

"So I assume you already know what hotel I was staying in?"

The man ignored her and looked back out at the skyline. Good. If she was an expert knife-thrower—sadly, her dad hadn't trained her for that—it could've been a window to go on offense. She just needed a longer opportunity. He was lowering his defenses. If only someone in the planes far above could see what was happening in the restaurant.

"Do you know someone at the hotel?" Matt asked. "I'd like to know."

The man still didn't answer. He continued staring across the room. What would take him off guard?

"You'll need me to enter the password to gain access to the computer," Isabelle said. "I would think you'd want my cooperation." She inhaled, searching the far reaches of her memory for verbiage she hoped would stall their demise.

He scoffed, "I doubt it." Finally she'd found a topic she could exploit.

"Okay, suit yourself, but you should know I used the Blum-Micali algorithm."

The operator raised one eyebrow. He stepped nearer. "The what?"

The closer he got, the better. "It's a cryptographically secure number generator," she said. "It can handle a quantum permanent compromise attack." She geared up to recite lengthy math equations, but the operator held up a hand.

"Hold on." He pressed his lips together and pulled out his phone. Good. He was distracted. It was now or never. She moved closer to Matt's ear. "Stay still," she whispered. She twisted her body as her hand slid across the countertop.

"She says she used an algorithm," the man said into the phone.

Isabelle grabbed the first thing her fingers found and pulled. It was the soda gun. Not ideal, but she'd work with what she had. She gave the metal tube a sharp tug, and her thumb slid over the red button labeled Coke, one of ten buttons on the button plate. She aimed at his face. Brown liquid and bubbles shot over Matt's shoulder and sprayed across the room.

"Are you kidding me?" The gunman growled as he held up the hand with the gun in front of his face.

She'd hoped for a more powerful distraction, but the soda sputtered to a trickle. Isabelle grabbed anything in arm's reach and began throwing it at the man: the metal shaker hit the guy's shoulder. As he lowered his arm,

Matt dived into his torso, sending him back over a table.

"Run," Matt yelled.

Isabelle watched Matt struggle to keep the man's corded arms back lest he aim the gun at either of them. Matt punched the man, and the gun fell from the operator's hand. Isabelle dashed toward it, but the guy was quick, shoving Matt back and flipping over onto the gun. Isabelle grabbed the nearest stool and hit the man's head with it.

He lay flat on his stomach with the gun underneath him. "Go," Matt shouted. It was too risky to try to wrestle the gun away, so this time she followed Matt's lead. Except they couldn't use the elevator since the operator had the key. Matt jumped over the body on the floor, grabbed her hand and pulled her around the corner to the door marked Stairs.

A gunshot sounded, and Matt shoved her head down as he slammed the door open with his elbow. The heat from the stairway overwhelmed her senses. The lack of air-conditioning meant it had to be over a hundred degrees between the cement walls.

Matt pulled on her wrist as another bullet pinged over her head. The man was coming.

They sprinted down the cement stairs. The

oppressive air made her breath shallow. "Faster, faster," Matt repeated.

Her ears strained, but she didn't hear any footsteps after them. No more bullets zinged past.

"What were you thinking?" Matt didn't slow his pace.

"Anything to keep him from killing us."

"Funny. Seems to me you almost got us killed."

"He was going to kill us no matter what, so I used OODA. Observe, Orient, Decide, Act. My dad taught me that."

"Sure he didn't say 'You bring the crazy, and Matt will bring the muscle'? Because that's what it felt like!"

She ignored him. She could've smarted back a number of comments, the bottom line being that they were still alive. If she didn't focus on the many steps below, the light-headed feeling starting to build in the back of her neck would overtake her. Sweat beaded on her forehead and ran down her cheek. Except for the sound of their panting and footsteps echoing off the stairs, there was nothing but silence. "Maybe he's not coming after us."

"Perhaps because he has an elevator and can block our exits," Matt replied. "He can beat us."

She hadn't thought of that. She slowed her

steps. What would they do? The floor numbers were marked in white paint. She snapped her fingers. "The party. Let's go back to the party."

"Where the guy who ordered to have you killed waits? Yeah, great idea."

"We don't know for sure if he was the one—" She wasn't ready to give up hope that Struther could be the answer to her problems.

"Izzy, he obviously set us up!"

"Maybe." It did seem like the most likely scenario. "Go to the party. There are loads of people still there, some talking, some waiting for the elevator. The gunman will think we're going to the bottom, right? To escape? Going to the party is unexpected. Safety in numbers."

Matt shook his head but didn't argue. He just kept moving down the stairs. Instead of sweat running down his temple, she noticed a streak of blood.

She almost stumbled, but her hand grabbed the railing to stop her descent. "He hurt you."

"Just a scratch." Matt jolted to a stop at the next platform. "I think this is it." He put his hand on the metal door. "Stay back. Let me see if our new friend is here." The door opened, and the smell of the chicken dinner they'd just eaten wafted past her. A group of conference attendees who'd gathered in front of the elevator spun around, slack-jawed at their appearance.

Robert Struther, at the far right of the group, raised an eyebrow. "Having a good time, Miss Barrows?"

Matt darted forward. "Stay away from her!" His hands tightened into fists, and his spine straightened.

Darren Allen took a step closer but said nothing.

"Someone call the police," Isabelle hollered, finally finding her voice again. She pointed a shaky finger at Struther. "Why would you try to kill me when I was willing to give you the research all along?"

Struther's eyes widened. "Ki-kill you? What are you talking about?"

"Oh, please." Matt took a step in front of Isabelle as if shielding her. "As if you don't know. Is your business doing so badly that you can't afford her? You have to steal instead?"

The crowd had grown utterly silent. "Did someone call the police?" Isabelle asked. One woman nodded, her phone pressed to her ear. "Tell them a gunman was in the building. He might've taken the elevator to the bottom. He's either almost out of the building..." She glanced at the metal door. "Or on his way back here."

The crowd reacted. Several let out gasps, some screamed, and then they dispersed throughout the room. It was probably the wrong thing to say. Only a couple of men remained near the elevator entrance, looking ready for a fight.

"Isabelle," Struther said. "What are you talking about?"

She faltered. Was there a possibility he wasn't behind it? "Let's just say our meeting didn't go as you intended. I'm still alive, and the research is safe."

His eyes clouded with confusion. "The elevator operator said the restaurant was closed. He said no one was going up. I thought you'd already gone back to your hotel. I promise." He held a hand up as if taking an oath. "I have witnesses." His expression pleaded for someone to corroborate his story.

Darren Allen shrugged. "Why don't you wait for the police to sort it out, Struther?" The way he said the last name indicated his great animosity for the man. Allen waved Isabelle toward the event room. "Let's get you away from the elevator." He lowered his voice. "I told you not to trust anyone."

The next time the elevator pinged, it held two police officers. "Ladies and gentlemen, we've got the Tower on lockdown until we can confirm you can leave safely."

Matt couldn't calm his racing heart. His eyes connected with Struther's as the officers interviewed him. One officer grabbed his radio pinned just below his collar. He spun around and found Isabelle. "We've found the gunman, outside waiting in the bushes."

Isabelle stood so close to Matt that her left arm brushed against his side as she shivered. Her chin dipped as she focused on the floor, her breathing rapid. Matt put an arm around her shoulders. "I'm fine. It's good you got him." She nodded rapidly. He could feel a slight tremor in her bones. "Thank you." She lifted her head. "What about the man at the hotel?"

The officer regarded Matt. "Your security is on the lookout, and we have officers doing a sweep. The front desk hasn't seen anyone as of yet. We'll have a car making rounds nearby tonight." He tilted his head. "My guess is now that we've got this guy, the attempted hotel burglary was called off."

Matt nodded. "Thank you." He pulled her closer into his side in an attempt to stop her shivering.

The officers informed the rest of the attendees that it was safe to leave.

Matt eyed Struther, still unsure of the guy's innocence, but if there was a chance he wasn't guilty… Matt sighed and walked forward. Struther tensed and pulled his chin back.

"It appears," Matt said slowly, "that I owe you an apology for how I spoke to you."

Struther's posture relaxed, but he crossed his arms across his chest. "I probably would've reacted the same way if someone held my girlfriend at gunpoint."

Isabelle joined them. "Oh, we're not—"

"Listen," Struther interjected. "I know it's not your fault, but I think it would be best if you partner with another company."

Her eyes widened. "But you haven't even heard what—"

"If your research is as valuable as it seems, then I'm sure you'll find another investor. I'm the new VP. Our company is just now stabilizing. We can't afford to become a target for... well, whoever is doing this. I'm sure you understand. I still look forward to your presentation." He nodded at them and walked away.

"I can't believe this is happening," Isabelle said.

"I know. I'm sorry." Matt glanced at his watch. "I hope our ride is still here."

"How'd you schedule a taxi already?"

"I prearranged something. I wanted transportation that could pull right up to the door since it's after dark."

The elevator dinged as if in response, and the crowd rushed into the metal box. Since they were the closest, Matt and Isabelle ended up pressed against the glass. He looked down at his feet and tried to ignore the feeling of his stomach trying to escape as they plummeted to the ground at an unreasonable speed. As it slowed to a stop, he looked up to find Isabelle beaming.

"The view of the city at night was beautiful. I needed that to help calm me. I wish you could've seen it." She touched his arm gently. "It means so much to me that you came. If the shoe was on the other foot and I was the one scared of heights, I don't think I could've done it."

He just hoped she wasn't ready to be rid of him, because there was no way he was letting Isabelle attend the conference tomorrow by herself. Only when she stepped through airport security on the way back home would he feel comfortable leaving her to fend for herself. Until tonight, there had been some part of him that still wanted to believe the acts of crime were coincidental. The gun and the attempt to get her laptop were on another level altogether.

Before the door had slid fully open, the attendees were rushing out, ignoring the operator's friendly goodbye. Matt didn't feel very friendly toward him, either. He could've been a little more specific that the restaurant was closed when they'd asked to go up the first time. "Did you know the other operator?" he asked now that they were the only ones left.

The guy shrugged. "No, but to be fair, I'm new here. I don't know everyone yet. I heard what happened. I would've warned you if I'd known."

Matt nodded. It made sense for the newbies to get stuck with the late-night private parties. It was what he would've done as manager. Seniority would give the other operators the cushier shifts.

"Thank you," Isabelle said.

They walked out onto the brick courtyard. The wind carried the powerful sound of the waterfall fountains directly across from the Tower. The light beaming from behind them made some of the water glow light green.

"It's hard to believe you can find so much beauty within the city." Isabelle's voice was as light and airy as the mist that reached their faces.

The air had cooled with the night, a welcome relief after the intense heat of the stairs. To the right of the massive fountains, a covered horse-drawn carriage waited. The carriage itself was draped in a few strands of white lights. The driver, dressed in a tuxedo, waved a few of the attendees away.

Matt grinned at Isabelle. "Our ride awaits. I'm glad he didn't give up on us."

She gasped. "That's for us?"

"He used to work for me. I helped him get this gig. He told me if I ever wanted a free ride... Well, I've never taken him up on it before." Mostly because he thought it'd feel awkward to be driven around town in a horse-drawn carriage all by himself by a guy he sometimes met for coffee.

It was a fully covered carriage except for the two small windows on either side. It had seemed like a safe enough idea before the gunman showed up. Now he wasn't so sure, though the cops seemed to think the danger had passed. He supposed that had to be good enough for now. The Tower had locked the doors behind him, and Matt didn't want to walk, exposed, to the parking lot and wait for a cab to arrive. Besides, the moment they got in the carriage, Bill would move them to the streets. There was safety in numbers.

"I can't wait," Isabelle exclaimed. She practically ran to the carriage entrance. She rose on her tiptoes to look at the driver. "I'm Isabelle," she said. "Thank you so much for doing this."

Bill tipped his hat to her. "Anything for Matt."

Isabelle placed one foot in the carriage but

looked over her shoulder at Matt. The affection written in her eyes took him off guard. He stepped closer to Bill. "We had a bit of a scare tonight. Any chance you drivers *carry* to keep from being robbed?"

Bill pointed to the cops leaving the scene. "I gathered something was going on." He patted his pocket. "I don't know about most drivers, but I'm trained and licensed. I'll deliver you safely."

Matt nodded, relieved. His chest tightened as he followed Isabelle inside the enclosed space. He'd thought they could sit across from each other, but instead there was only one small padded bench. It'd be impossible not to be in close proximity. They barely had sat down before the clip-clop of hooves started.

Isabelle kept her eyes on the views outside the window. "I can't imagine a better way to take in the sights."

"Well, you really haven't had a chance to see much," Matt said. And sadly, until he was absolutely sure she was no longer in danger, he didn't feel like she could. "I imagine, though, that Bill will take the scenic route to the hotel."

Bill didn't disappoint. They passed the numerous notable buildings on the way back, and Matt recited what history he knew. Otherwise, the sound of passing cars and horse hooves were all that filled the silence. The glow of the lights lit Isabelle's face and the highlights of her hair. He'd never thought it possible for her to grow more beautiful.

She turned toward him. He moved his gaze past her and pointed at the river just beyond the bridge they were crossing.

"The San Antonio River used to be called Yanaguana, 'place of restful waters.'"

Her eyebrows rose. "Oh? I always like knowing what names mean."

"Do you know your name means 'God is my oath'?"

She nodded. "Or 'devoted to God.' It's a good reminder to me when I forget my purpose."

"Hard to believe you'd ever forget. You've always seemed driven, just like the other Isabel Barrows."

Her eyes widened. "You know about her?"

SEVEN

Isabelle didn't know what to say. How would he know what her name meant or the fact that a woman in history had the same name unless he'd looked her up on the internet at some point?

"First woman employed by the State Department, right?" Matt asked.

"Uh, yeah, among other things. First female ophthalmologist, eye surgeon, professor at a medical school... Let's just say I'm glad my first name is spelled differently."

"You should be proud of what you've accomplished. You're well on your way, Isabelle."

The compliment took her so off guard that she turned back to the open window and the breeze. "I don't know about that. After tonight, every investor will treat me like I've got the plague. And if I don't find one, I'll have let Hank down, and my livelihood will be at stake, as well."

"Don't give up. You have a new home that sounds like it's worth fighting for."

"It's what I always wanted."

"I know. So, what about Struther? I'm not so sure you should trust him."

"Funny. That's what Darren Allen said before we headed to the restaurant."

Matt narrowed his eyes. "That's a little suspicious. Wasn't it Struther and Allen we saw arguing outside the restaurant yesterday?"

She turned back to the window. They were passing the Alamo, lit up in all its glory. "Yes, but, Matt, I don't want to think about it anymore. I can't make sense of it, and I don't have any evidence for the police. So I just want to be a tourist on a moonlit carriage ride and soak it all in." She sighed. For all her talk, she couldn't stop her mind from spinning. "Besides, I'm realizing that almost every attendee at the conference could find a way to profit from my research. I really can't trust anyone."

Matt placed his palm on top of her hand. "Except me." His touch almost took her breath away.

She smiled while trying to tame her racing heart and shallow breathing. "Except you." Her words slipped past her tight throat in a whisper. The sights of San Antonio no longer held her interest. She couldn't bring herself to look away from Matt's caring gaze, and she didn't want to move a muscle to break contact, even though she knew she should.

There was no good that could come from falling for Matt. He didn't think of her that way, and even if that somehow changed, they both had busy, demanding lives thousands of miles apart.

The carriage jolted and came to a halt.

Matt's hand disappeared. "Looks like our time is up."

She turned to face the bright lights of the hotel entryway and hoped his words weren't true in more ways than one.

Matt approached the reservation desk and made sure no one had tried to find out Isabelle's room number. If anyone were watching them, it would appear as if she was making sure no one had accessed the main hotel safe.

After confirming there'd been no inquiries, they walked toward the elevators in silence. Once inside, they turned around and looked out at the empty marble lobby, spotting a familiar figure slouched into the couch. His arms were folded and his chin rested against his chest.

"Isn't that—"

Matt smacked a hand against the side of the elevator door, shoving them back open. "Mr. Frazer? Yeah. It appears he's fallen asleep." He stepped back into the lobby. "Sorry, Isabelle. I need to take care of this. Think you'll get to your room okay?"

She nodded when what she really wanted to do was shake her head. As the doors closed and the elevator made its way up to her room, the loneliness proved almost suffocating. It was easier to ignore the events of the week when someone else was with her. And she still was without a cell phone to keep her occupied.

The doors slid open, and her heart raced as she leaned forward and peeked to the left and the right down the hallway. She detected nothing but the hum of a soda machine at the far end. No longer caring if she looked stupid, she ran until she reached her room, shoved the card into the reader and slammed the door behind her.

The room lights were still on, just as she'd left them. She stepped no farther. Instead she bent down to see if the folded gum wrapper was still on the spot she'd left it. Satisfied, she checked the dresser. The broken toothpick was also where she'd left it. It appeared no one had been in her room.

Matt was downstairs. She was safe. She could sleep.

Her body didn't want to listen to her, though. She still couldn't inhale fully, which only stressed her out more. Her entire body began to shake, and her throat tightened. She would not cry, though. She was better than that. She could handle it. She'd been raised—trained, really—for moments like these.

Okay, she wasn't specifically prepared for her life to be in danger, her entire career to be hanging by a thread and the attraction to Matt to return with a terrifying renewed vigor. But her dad had taught her how to handle stress. Deep breath in for five seconds, deep breath out for five seconds…and her stomach gurgled. Great. She was starving.

As she dived into her suitcase, hoping there was still a granola bar in the zippered compartment, reality hit her in the gut. Someone wanted her research, and they wanted her gone. And even if she went home with her tail between her legs without an investor, failure wouldn't come with assurances the threat would be gone. She sank onto her mattress, defeated and no longer hungry. If she didn't find the culprit soon, she'd end up dead either way.

Matt stood in front of the sleeping Mr. Frazer. Maybe the man wasn't looking for a place to host an event at all. Maybe he was actually homeless, and that was why he'd been in the hotel last night, as well. Matt took a deep breath and sat next to him on the leather couch. "Mr. Frazer?"

The man jostled and straightened. He chuckled. "I'm so sorry. I took advantage of your free coffee. I ordered decaf, but maybe I should've ordered high octane." He stood. "Well, I'll be off."

Matt wasn't sure what to say lest he offend the man, so he watched him leave the lobby. The security cameras were located in the corners. Had they caught any strange men casing the hotel's safe while Matt and Isabelle were held at gunpoint? He strolled to the security guard's office. "Can you show me the footage from an hour ago?"

Connor, the guard for the night shift, nodded. "Yes, sir."

If Matt found anyone who looked like a thief getting ready to break into the hotel's safe, he would call the police. Time ticked by slowly as they ran through video showcasing different angles. The footage was grainy, but aside from people moving in and out of the lobby and Mr. Frazer slouched on the couch, there wasn't any behavior of note. Maybe when the gunman had called someone about passwords as Isabelle aimed soda—Matt shook his head at the memory—it had scared off the impending robbery before it happened.

"I want all staff to be on alert for any unusual behavior, though."

"Yes, sir."

Paranoia might have made him overly cautious. Matt thanked Connor and headed straight for the front desk.

He lifted his badge out of the cubby underneath the counter and slipped it on. When he worked in an official capacity, he wanted to make it known. Since he lived in the hotel, as well, the employees knew he was on the clock when the badge said so.

And since he planned to accompany Isabelle the following day, he needed to work ahead and make preparations for the nursing conference tomorrow to ensure his employees had all the information they needed for the event to run smoothly.

Ellen, a longtime employee, worked quietly on the nightly audit reports.

Soothing melodies played softly through the lobby speakers. Otherwise there was nothing but silence. The adrenaline had kept him going while looking over security footage and preparing for the conference, but when Matt's eyelids grew heavy, he glanced at the clock. Two in the morning. He'd be worthless to Isabelle if he didn't get some sleep.

The elevator dinged.

Since no one had entered the lobby, it meant someone was coming down from the rooms. Usually it was tourists who had indulged in too much Texan food for their uninitiated stomachs to handle. "Got the antacids handy?"

Ellen didn't even look up from the lines of numbers on her screen. She held her hand up with the rolled package of Tums in her hand. "Not my first rodeo."

The doors slid open. Isabelle stood, barefoot and clad in pink striped pajamas. Head down and hair mussed, she staggered into the lobby and down the nearest hallway toward the twenty-four-hour fitness center.

"What on earth?" Ellen asked.

"I've got this." Matt followed her. How was he supposed to keep her safe if she was going to roam the hotel in the middle of the night? He'd told her specifically to stay behind closed doors.

Isabelle shuffled to the door to the fitness center, pushed the hotel key into the card reader and disappeared behind the door. Something was off. Going to the gym at two in the morning, barefoot, didn't compute. Matt lengthened his stride to catch up.

Through the glass door he could see Isabelle standing still on the treadmill, her expression slack but seemingly staring at the lone man doing crunches on a mat while he watched baseball replays on the television mounted from the ceiling. The man turned his head mid-crunch, as if noticing Isabelle for the first time. He lurched upright into a sitting position.

Matt opened the door. "She's sleepwalking."

Isabelle didn't react. The man turned to him, registering Matt's name tag. He sighed. "Good. I was about to get worried," he whispered.

"You don't have to be quiet. I'll escort her out."

"I was done with my workout anyway." The muscle-bound man picked up one of the hotel's gym towels and flung it over his shoulder. "It's dangerous to wake up a sleepwalker."

"That's a myth," Matt muttered as the man left the fitness center. Isabelle didn't move a muscle. He'd had no idea she still struggled with the condition.

He'd never forget the time his mom had found her the night before high-school finals week, making a turkey sandwich in his family's kitchen at three in the morning. After that, they decided they probably shouldn't leave a hide-a-key on the porch. Isabelle had known where it was since she'd watered their plants when they were on vacation. Her parents had also installed an alarm so they would know when she tried to leave in the middle of the night.

Matt approached her from the side of the treadmill. "Isabelle." He placed a hand gently on her arm while placing his other hand behind her back in case she startled. "Isabelle, honey, wake up."

She turned to look at him. Her forehead squinted with confusion before her entire face flushed with fear. Her body shuddered.

"It's okay. You're okay."

Her eyes wide, she looked around. "Where am I?" She took shallow, rapid breaths.

"Come here. There's a bench here. Why don't you sit down?" He led her gently until they were side by side. "You still sleepwalk?"

She dropped her head into her hands. "I didn't think so." She looked up at her surroundings. "I mean, not in ages. Though I don't remember unless someone tells me. And even when I was younger, it was only when I was super stressed out." Her mouth dropped open.

That explained it.

Isabelle cringed. "I'm sorry. I fell asleep worrying. And after tonight…" She rubbed her temples.

Matt didn't need an explanation. Truth be told, he probably didn't need to work so much tonight, but he wasn't sure he could fall asleep, either.

"Did anyone see me?"

"One man thought you were stalking him."

Isabelle gaped. "You're teasing." She laughed as she caught sight of the game on television. "Besides, I'm not into sports."

He laughed halfheartedly. "Clearly some part of you is."

She frowned. "What do you mean?"

"Nothing. Only it seems a little odd that you said liking the football star was just an attempt to get my attention, but then you up and dated him...for years."

One eyebrow lifted. "I don't really see the connection, but I can tell you that when a handsome guy shows interest in you despite being warned off—in very unflattering terms, I might add—it feels nice." Her eyebrows scrunched closer. "Besides, why do you care? We dated. It was fun. Never serious."

"It must've been serious if he asked you to move away with him."

"He wasn't devastated that I said no. We weren't some hot item. It wasn't leading to marriage. We were just friends who also dated."

"Just friends, huh? Like we were friends?"

She scrunched up her mouth and stood up, hands on her hips. "You can't seriously be mad about this." Isabelle's shoulders dropped, and her expression softened. "Are you?"

He couldn't stop himself. He wanted to make

his mouth stop. Just stop. The exhaustion and the fight with the gunman had taken more of a toll on his self-control than he'd realized. The emotion welled up in his chest until it burst. "I liked you, okay? Back then, I said all those things to Randy because I wanted you for myself. I know it was wrong and immature, and I should've told you right away at dinner last night. But I didn't." Like a tire leaking air, his words rushed out until he was left deflated.

She took a step backward and looked up at the ceiling. "Wow." She exhaled. "That's—" A small laugh escaped. "We were quite a pair. A couple of chickens."

He blew out a breath. "Lying chickens." He hung his head. She was crediting him with more grace than he deserved. "I'm sorry it came out that way. It'd been weighing on me. I needed to confess, and I need to ask your forgiveness."

"Given." She lowered onto the bench beside him. "I'm glad you told me, even when we're both a bit loopy from sleep deprivation."

Matt hung his head. He'd never been so tired.

"And I'm glad we're not teens anymore. I made so many stupid mistakes back then." She punched his shoulder lightly. "So we can put all that behind us and be friends again. I've missed your friendship."

Her voice sounded light and airy, tickling his eardrums. Wait. Friendship? He was about to confess that his attraction and admiration had only grown, and instead, he'd been friend-zoned. His pride could not handle another blow. "Yes. Well, we've got an early morning tomorrow, so…"

She yawned and stretched, almost on cue. "I hope I can go back to sleep. If you hadn't stopped me…"

He stood and took her hand to pull her back to standing. "Don't worry about it. I'll make sure no one lets you walk into harm's way." Although he had yet to figure out how. There was too much at stake to leave the responsibility with his overnight skeleton crew.

She smiled up at him with a peaceful, sleepy and trusting gaze. His heart almost flipped out of his chest. As he walked her back to the elevator, he debated if he could hire extra security staff while staying within budget. Since there wasn't a proven, active threat on the hotel guests, it'd be hard to justify. Even if he pulled it off, his boss at corporate would object.

Isabelle turned around at her door. "Good night, Matt."

Matt nodded. He took the elevator back down to the lobby. Only one solution presented itself. Ellen stood, holding the antacids in one hand. Matt waved at her and dragged the closest wingback chair into the elevator.

His back sent out a warning twinge as he carried the chair—pulling it across the hallway might wake guests—until he reached Isabelle's door. He carefully placed the wingback right in front of it and sat down with a sigh. Morning wasn't too many hours away, but spending the night in the chair would make for a long one.

"Sleeping on the job, huh?" a gruff voice asked.

Matt jolted in the chair. His neck and back screamed at the quick change in position. He blinked and looked at his watch. Six in the morning already?

The older man chuckled as he escorted his wife past Matt's station.

"Why would he be here?" the woman asked her husband. She pressed the elevator button.

"How should I know?"

"Maybe he's guarding someone." She gasped. "A celebrity or a royal?" She leaned back and flashed an expectant look at Matt.

Matt stood at attention and tried his best to flash a smile that probably looked more like a sneer. "It's hotel policy not to divulge the identity of our guests, ma'am."

The wife elbowed her husband. "Wait until

Marge hears about this. She's gonna wish she'd stayed with us."

Matt turned his back to the couple and rubbed his face awake. He prayed the Lord would hear him and keep danger away from Isabelle, because at the moment, Matt was no good to anyone. He was dead on his feet.

EIGHT

No. Everyone—or at least half her list of prospective investors—said no. They were more polite than that, but the result was the same. Her research and institute were synonymous with "risk we can't afford right now." In other words, they didn't want anyone targeting them.

And yet everyone she had talked to indicated they couldn't wait for her presentation. Perhaps that meant they were hoping to figure out the trigger to tracking her research for themselves. She'd have to omit the story about what inspired her to think of the idea, in case their minds worked the same way.

Sandra Parveen, the conference organizer, had been accommodating to her request to allow Matt access and even a boxed dinner. It was a good thing, since Matt refused to leave her alone anymore. Most conferences would've refused, but Parveen had gushed instead. "Consider it a presenter perk. We might want favors from Matt someday."

Isabelle hoped that wasn't the case.

As if she knew Isabelle had been replaying the conversation in her mind, Sandra approached while Isabelle stood in line for the boxed dinners.

"Hank called me this afternoon for an update." Sandra Parveen had a conspiratorial tone to her voice. "He was very upset after hearing about the Tower incident last night."

Isabelle groaned. Hank didn't need any more stress. There was a reason—besides not having a phone—she hadn't kept Hank updated on the attempts. "But you told him the gunman was arrested, right? I'm perfectly safe."

Sandra waved Isabelle's concern away. "Of course, but he wanted to make sure you had transportation back to the hotel tonight. His treat. I'm supposed to let you know that he already scheduled a cab to pick you up once the evening session is over."

"Oh. That's thoughtful. Thank you." It was just like her uncle to do something like that. Even though his finances were already tight.

Isabelle walked past a group of chatting marine biologists. This particular day of the conference was a highlight because the extra classes and workshops lasted into the evening.

Thankfully they provided dinner. She had tried to talk Matt into going back to the hotel when she realized how long a day it would be, but he refused.

She rounded the corner and spotted him, sitting in the lobby of the conference center. He didn't see her, though. In his business suit, he blended in with the rest of the professionals. She slowed her steps so she could stare longer.

The odd thing about sleepwalking was that she never recalled what she'd done, no matter how hard she struggled to recollect. But she remembered everything after Matt had woken her up on the treadmill. She'd been fully awake for the conversation in the fitness center, but it had seemed like a dream. Every tiny detail, even the ones she wanted to forget, like the state of her hair, had seared into her conscious.

Across the room, the overhead lights highlighted his bronze hair and trimmed beard over what she knew to be a chiseled jaw. His lips were slightly pouty and his forehead wrinkled as he jotted in a notebook in a leather portfolio. She'd seen the expression before when he'd been studying.

If she asked him a question in the middle of his thoughts, no doubt it would take him a good ten seconds to answer. The funny thing was, he teased her about the same trait. Once she entered a laser-like focus zone, it proved difficult to escape.

Matt glanced up and tapped his pen to his chin. He stared directly at her, unseeing, deep in thought. Still, she quickened her steps so she wouldn't be caught looking.

"Barrows," a voice bellowed.

She flinched and turned around.

Darren Allen pointed at her as he sauntered in her direction. "I'm beginning to feel like the only belle at the ball who hasn't been asked for a dance."

"Excuse me?" She asked the question with a smile plastered on her face. If there were an actual dance scheduled during the conference, she'd feel no remorse skipping the event.

"You haven't asked me for a meeting about investing."

She pursed her lips. "Uh, I didn't think your nonprofit invested in private research."

He shoved his hands in his pockets. "True, true. But I like to foster relationships for the benefit of the cause. I know people...connections that I can arrange for you. I would like to hear what your research has uncovered."

Movement behind her made her spin around. Matt stood at her side, one hand placed lightly at her back. He said nothing but offered her a small smile. She turned to Mr. Allen again.

"Um...well, I need to attend the rest of the workshops. What about tomorrow? Perhaps at lunch?"

He nodded, ignoring Matt. "Lunch it is." He strode off without a word.

"You're seriously going to meet with Mr. Trust No One?"

She handed Matt his boxed dinner. "I know it sounds bad, but I can't afford to disregard him. He is a big mover and shaker in the industry."

"You can't afford to misjudge him, either." Matt sighed. "As soon as we're done here, we're picking you up some protection."

"It's not like I can get a gun at the drugstore."

Matt's eyes widened. "No, but you can get a prepaid phone, for starters. I know you want to wait until you're back home to put your spare phone on your plan, but it's not safe to be without any form of communication."

He had a point. And it would be useful to be able to call Hank more often. Maybe he could get her some more cash or a prepaid Visa so she wouldn't have to rely on Matt so much. "Fair enough."

"And I'll see what I can do about the rest. What if you spoke with that Allen guy over the phone?"

She leaned forward, processing what he'd said. "When we'll be eating lunch in the same room tomorrow? Just a hunch, but it might come across as snubbing him."

"If he's overly sensitive, maybe."

She gave her head a little shake. "I'm still jumpy after the Tower incident. Believe me, I don't want to take any unnecessary risks, but I can't afford to alienate the one person who might help save my job."

He pulled back. "Save your job?"

She bit her lip. She'd said too much. "That might be exaggerating."

"Izzy?"

"I told you Hank has dipped into his own retirement. He hasn't said my job is on the line, but he spent all the extra money on upgrading our data security. If I don't bring in any investors, I don't see how he can keep going, and I'll feel like it's all my fault."

"Maybe you should ask him. A good businessman plans for things to go wrong."

She wasn't even sure how she'd start such a conversation. Besides, it was her uncle, and it seemed like her responsibility to make sure he wouldn't need to worry about such things.

"This is about your job," Matt said. "If he's a professional then it won't bother him."

Maybe he had a point, but she didn't want to rock the boat. She never wanted Hank to regret hiring her. And how likely was it that her uncle had a backup plan if he had dipped into his retirement already?

Besides, she refused to consider moving or starting over again. Ever. Last night's revelations further highlighted why she hated going from one place to another. If she hadn't moved away to South Carolina, maybe she and Matt would've overcome the hurt and pride and revealed their feelings for each other years ago instead of after a sleepwalking adventure gone wrong. They would've never moved on from their feelings, and instead the attraction might've grown, might've blossomed, might've led to love and…

"Isabelle?"

She blinked. "Huh?"

"I asked if you wanted to eat. Must've been thinking about something good, judging by your dreamy smile."

Heat rushed up her neck. "I heard they put brownies in the box."

He laughed and waved her to the seat beside him. "Glad to know some things haven't changed."

If he only knew.

He opened the box lid. "Oh. Tuna salad. Haven't had this in a while."

"You've got to be kidding me." Her stomach flipped a little at the thought.

"What's the problem?"

"I don't eat seafood."

His mouth was already full, and the smell of onions and tuna hit her. "Since when?"

She opened the bag of nacho chips. "Since I started working in marine biology."

Matt waved at everyone else. "Doesn't seem to be bothering them."

"Well, I'm not everyone else, am I? In some nations it's the only food source, and that's fine, but not in the US. They're the wildlife of the sea."

He raised an eyebrow with a half smile growing. "That sounds well prepared but totally not the Izzy I know. What's the real reason?"

She sighed. He was the only person who knew her younger self well enough to call her out. "Fine. It sounds better than telling everyone I don't want to eat what I look at all day. It sounds…immature."

He laughed and winked. "I'll keep your secret."

She pointed at his portfolio. "What about you? I think a secret deserves a secret. What are you working on?"

He sighed. "My ideal work environment."

"You don't have that now? Aside from the occasional guest who puts you in mortal danger?"

He picked up the portfolio. "Things I would

love to implement when I get the chance with my own place."

"Your own place? You can't implement whatever you want here?" She'd thought he loved his job. He took so much pride in it. She assumed he felt the same way she did about wanting a forever home, somewhere to settle down. After all, he grew up in the same house for his entire life before he left for college. Wouldn't he want that again?

"No. A national corporation owns the hotel. And while I'm able to make tweaks, it can never be what I truly want—a place that puts Christian values above making a profit." He sighed. "My brother David is building a new conference center near Pismo Beach. It seems like the perfect time to show my family what I can do so that maybe I can take over the management portion."

California. She should've known he'd want to move closer to home. And while it was closer to Oregon, a drive to Pismo Beach would still be over thirteen hours, so not feasible for a decent relationship, even a long-distance one. She shoved a chip in her mouth to snap her mind out of going there.

"So, your entire family is coming here to do an interview of sorts?" She didn't understand. They knew he was competent and had the degree and education. Did he really need to convince them?

"No, I told them to come here on vacation." He glanced at her. "Which it is," he added hastily. "I'm just hoping they see I could really benefit their operation."

"But they have no idea you even want the job?"

He shrugged. "Technically, no."

She recognized the way he pulled his shoulders back. Matt's pride was almost as strong as his biceps. She also remembered that when Matt set his jaw a certain way, it meant he didn't want anyone's opinion, and the matter was closed for discussion. Pulling his shoulders back was a precursor to the jaw move, which meant he was still listening and hadn't shut her out quite yet.

"You need to tell them you want the job."

"It's already a family business. Everyone is involved but me. If they want me then they need to ask me."

"What do you mean, everyone?"

Matt held his hand out and ticked off each finger. "Dad and David are both in construction. Luke is a developer, so he can give them advice on franchising and expanding, and James is a computer genius, so he's setting up their intranet and customized booking software."

"But if they think you love it here, how will they know—"

His jaw clenched. He pointed at the other attendees. "Looks like they're leaving for the next session. You don't want to miss out."

She stared into his eyes, and as they softened, she couldn't help but think she'd already missed out.

Matt looked at his watch. At this rate, the stores would be closed before they could purchase her pepper spray and a cheap phone. At the sight of Isabelle walking through the throng of attendees toward him, his shoulders relaxed while his gut tightened. When they'd spoken at dinner, a course of electricity had run through his body whenever she looked at him. A fire in her eyes that drew him closer...that made him think of pulling her into his arms and kissing her for the first time.

Isabelle waved at him. Matt averted his gaze to the taxis outside so he could compose his features and capture his thoughts. "Boy, that was a long day," she said. "But totally worth it. You really didn't have to stay this whole time—"

"Izzy, we've been over this. I wanted to." Had her eyes somehow gotten bluer over the last hour? Matt sighed. "We need to hurry."

"Oh, I forgot to tell you. Hank ordered us a taxi."

They stepped out onto the sidewalks. The air, heavy with moisture, slowed his breathing and forced his heart rate to slow down. The day was almost done, and he couldn't wait to relax in his room and sleep…except for the small matter of Isabelle's sleepwalking. He hadn't figured out that problem yet. After a full day without any excitement, perhaps it wasn't a risk tonight.

Isabelle leaned past him to peek around his shoulder at the cabs lined up at the curb. He inhaled and a light mixture of vanilla and violets wafted past him. How—after such a long day—could she still smell so good?

"Look. That cabdriver is standing outside his car. What if he's waiting for us?"

"Probably." Matt resisted taking her hand as they walked toward him.

"Barrows?" the man asked.

Isabelle grinned. "Yes. Thank you."

Matt opened the door for Isabelle before the driver had a chance. He walked around the car and took a seat behind the driver's. "Please take us to the pharmacy on Commerce before we go to the hotel."

The driver nodded and pulled into traffic.

"Matt, you don't have to do this."

It hurt Isabelle's pride to lean on other people. He understood that, probably better than most. But she needed a phone and some means of self-defense. "If it makes you feel better, you can pay me back when you get home." Or at least try. That should ease her mind, but for Matt, it meant she'd have to call or email him once she got home. Then he would insist it was a gift. He'd be prepared by then with an interesting topic of discussion, and they would debate like normal, like the good ole days.

Isabelle pursed her lips. "Oh. Okay. I guess that'd work." She sighed. "I hate being broke."

Matt laughed. "I understand the feeling."

The driver turned on Market Street. Matt hated when people told drivers how to do their job, especially when there were one-way streets and traffic patterns to consider, but this would take them in the opposite direction, toward the freeway.

Matt leaned forward. "I think you misunderstood. We want the corner of Commerce and Navarro."

"Different way."

Matt figured he'd say something like that. The meter caught his eye. "You didn't start your fare."

"Paid for."

Isabelle also leaned forward, eyes wide. "Oh, but I actually care that my boss doesn't pay too much. Please start it. I'll make a note of how much it costs." Her voice remained light and airy, but her tightened forehead revealed the restrained irritation.

The driver slapped the little black box and the red numbers indicated the fare had begun. Matt didn't take kindly to cabdrivers making a bad name for the other hardworking drivers in the area. All it took was one guy overpricing.

Matt looked for the license so he could report him later. He had a few contacts in the city, so he felt certain he'd be taken seriously. The darkness in the cab made it hard to see, though. The streetlights reflected off the plastic covering the cabdriver's identification. He squinted. The shape of the man's face on the ID didn't quite match the driver's. Had the man recently lost weight?

The light reflected again, but this time a beam bounced off something metallic tucked underneath the man's right leg. The driver dragged his hand to cover it but kept one hand on the steering wheel.

A gun.

Matt pulled back. He needed to remain calm. At face value, there was nothing to get upset about. San Antonio had an open carry law, though it seemed unwise and unlikely that a driver would actually hold the weapon while driving. They still drove in the opposite direction of the pharmacy. Only a couple more stoplights and they would be out of the tourist area and closer to the freeway.

"I changed my mind," Matt said. "I want to go to Las Ramblas Restaurant." They had just passed Hotel Contessa, where it was located. "You can drop us off here."

The driver made no motion to stop. Isabelle's eyes widened as she darted looks between Matt and the driver. "Pull over!"

"Listen, lady. Hush up and enjoy the ride." The driver held up the gun and waved it at them. His menacing glare connected with Matt in the rearview mirror. "No sudden moves."

Isabelle's right hand was flicking her fingers in dramatic shapes at him. As if she was trying to communicate something with her hands. Her pinkie finger swung around, she pointed up, she made a fist, and then she pointed down. It vaguely registered as sign language, but he didn't know what it meant. She jutted her chin forward and blinked hard at him as if that would help him understand.

The driver kept glancing up at him in the rearview mirror. Which meant he'd catch Matt if he tried to pull out a phone from inside his suit jacket. Matt gripped his black leather portfolio hard. The man would have a hard time shooting at them from the angle of the driver's seat. They could try to jump out and roll while moving, but even at a slower speed, without padding, their clothes would be shredded. Isabelle wore a sleeveless blouse, so her shoulders would take most of the impact. Plus the risk of the cars in the adjacent lanes running over them was high.

"Who hired you?" Isabelle demanded. "We'll pay you double."

"After you were complaining about being broke." The driver cackled as he pulled up to a red light. "Nice try, sweetheart."

He'd lowered his guard. Matt swung the portfolio as hard as he could into the back of the guy's head. The driver's head smashed into the steering wheel, and the car screeched to a stop. "Run," Matt yelled.

NINE

Isabelle didn't need to be told twice. She flung the car door open and jumped out as she heard Matt grunt. She spun to check on him and met the driver's dark eyes. He lifted his arm, holding the gun. His shirt gaped, revealing a tattoo down the right side of his neck and down over his chest. Matt smacked the weapon hard with his portfolio.

She didn't wait to see if he succeeded in knocking it out of the man's hand. She ran to the sidewalk. Matt sprinted toward her as another cabdriver jumped out of the car in the lane parallel to theirs. Except the look on the other driver's face gave her chills. He didn't ask if she was all right. Instead he charged, lifting his arm.

Crack!

Matt's hand grabbed hers and yanked as she ducked. Brick pieces shattered around her. They darted around the corner of the building.

Matt pushed her behind the decorative trees. She let him pull her through the landscaping until they reached a metal bridge, except they didn't go across. He veered right and they raced down curved steps.

Not again. What if the two guys with guns managed to corner them? But Matt was leading and knew the area. They reached what looked like another section of the River Walk. Across from the river, a dim glow from within glass walls looked like a restaurant, Las Ramblas. Except she didn't see any diners. It was late on a weeknight.

"I wish the stairs led to that side of the river," Matt mumbled. "We could've run into the restaurant. There's not much for a while." He kept his hand gripped around her palm, pulling her slightly.

They jogged past empty benches. "What was with the extreme gesturing?"

"Gesturing?" Oh. The sign language. "I was telling you we should jump out of the car."

"How would I know that's what you meant?"

"Ninth grade. We learned the alphabet in sign language."

"You're unbelievable. I don't remember any of that."

She huffed. Jogging wasn't a normal part of her workout routine. They ran underneath the bridge, and Matt slowed to a walk. The darkness enveloped them enough that Isabelle dared a look back. The two men were sprinting in their direction, rushing up a ramp that would take them to the bridge above them. The men would be able to spot, aim and shoot from that vantage point. In other words, they were trapped.

"Isabelle," Matt whispered. He pulled her close to the river, next to an edge without a railing. If he expected her to jump into the river, she'd rather face bullets. Okay, not really, but the water didn't look the cleanest, and she dreaded the thought of jumping in.

He pointed ahead. A boat filled with laughing tourists was headed their way.

"But it's headed the way we just came," she said.

He nodded as he pulled off his jacket. "Exactly." He slipped it on her shoulders as he waved dramatically at the Rio Taxi driver.

She thrust her arm toward the bridge above their heads. "Those men are up there. They will see us."

"And any minute, they'll decide we're hiding underneath the bridge. Either way, we need to get out. We get on and we blend in. Act like we're part of a group. Wear the jacket. We need to cover up any identifying factors."

In other words, she needed to cover up her clothes. She pulled the jacket tight around her torso. The heat and the jacket didn't pair well, but at least it held a mixture of forest smells: juniper, jasmine, cedar and fir. She almost asked what cologne he used. The boat slowed down and pulled over.

"Can't you pull up your hair?" he asked.

"With what?" She had nothing without her handy messenger bag.

"Get in quick, or they might suspect." He grabbed her hand and pulled her into the middle of the boat before it'd fully stopped. He stepped over legs of tourists, still holding her hand, so that she was forced to follow him. He handed the driver the cash.

He took a seat, squeezed in between two women who were forced to scoot over for Isabelle. "Sorry, sorry," she repeated. Isabelle glanced at the bags on many of the laps. They were with some kind of conference for nurses. She remembered seeing a sign about it in the lobby of the hotel.

"Great place for a conference, right? Couldn't have picked a better hotel," Isabelle said. "Did you have the breakfast parfait this morning?"

The women's eyes widened with assumption that they were also nurses. "Oh, I had the quiche, but my friend tried it. What'd you think about the keynote?"

Oh. Well, Isabelle couldn't answer that question, and the tip of the boat had already passed the bridge. They were about to be in the open. "Isabelle." She turned around. Matt's right arm came around her shoulder and reached for the back of her hair.

"What are you doing?"

He leaned close and balled up her hair until it felt like it was all gathered at the nape of her neck. "Trying to hide your hair," he whispered into her ear. "And we need to hide our faces."

That was going to be awkward after the group of nurses was waiting for her answer on the keynote. Plus a couple hiding their faces in a group of mostly women…yeah, that seemed out of place. How could they blend in and keep hidden? Her eyes widened. "Ask me to marry you. Loudly."

"Will you marry me?" Matt asked, his face slack.

The group gasped. "Yes," Isabelle answered quickly.

Shouts of exclamation and clapping surrounded them. Sometimes the easiest way to hide was to cause a scene. The gunmen wouldn't suspect them to be a part of a loud, obnoxious party. As their boat slipped out into the open air, Matt's left arm pulled her close and his lips covered her mouth.

The whoops and hollers surrounding her faded in the background. In the back of her mind, she knew there was a possibility the gunmen could still spot them, so she leaned into the kiss, hiding their faces from view. At least, that was what she would tell herself later. His lips tasted like the chocolate after-dinner mint in their box. His trimmed beard brushed against her chin, but it didn't bother her. Instead it seemed to awaken her senses. She slipped her hands up his arms, past his shoulders, to his neck.

His right hand still held her hair, almost cradling her head. The ladies seemed to be talking louder than ever over the birds cawing from the trees and the splashing of the water against the hull of the boat.

"Ladies and gentlemen," a voice boomed through speakers nearby, "the romantic lure of the River Walk brings two people together once again."

The nurses were agreeing, talking to the driver and each other. Many of them exclaimed their intention to bring their spouses next time.

Matt broke the kiss but leaned his forehead against hers. He looked into her eyes for the briefest of moments, and Isabelle went soft. She didn't think she could get up and run away even if she tried. Matt's eyes darted to the side and upward. "I think it worked," he whispered.

"You'll have a good story," the lady next to her said. "So romantic. How long have you two known each other?"

"Sometimes it feels like only a moment. Other times, it feels like forever," Matt said.

Isabelle scrunched her nose. What was that supposed to mean?

He waved at the driver. "Could we get off at the next stop?"

The man handed Matt two tickets with a wink. "You bought the day pass. You can get on any of the other taxis for the rest of the day."

Isabelle couldn't relax despite the fact that their trick got them away from the gunmen. The fake proposal had been her idea, as a distraction, but she'd never imagined he'd kiss her. It would be the natural thing following a marriage proposal, she supposed. It was good thinking on his part.

Her breath shook as she processed the events of the last minute. Matt McGuire kissed her. No, it didn't seem real. She didn't want to admit just how many times she'd hoped he would. But she hadn't thought a kiss could hold so much...meaning. Except it was pretend. And she needed to remember that. Otherwise any future man in her life, any first kiss, would forever be compared to *that* kiss. One thing was certain… Matt had missed his calling in life. The man should've been an actor.

The boat curved with the river, and they headed north instead of west. It slid to an exit point on the left side, just past the Republic of Texas Restaurant. Matt hopped onto the sidewalk and reached down for her hand. The nurses hooted and hollered their wishes for a romantic night. Isabelle waved them away as Matt guided her toward another set of stairs.

His head swiveled from side to side, eyes alert. "I'm so on edge, I forgot I have a new phone. It's in my jacket. Could you give it to me?"

Isabelle slipped off the jacket and handed it back to him. He could get the phone himself. If she wore it much longer, she'd resemble a steamed lobster. Besides, she could do without the reminder of his smell, no matter how pleasant. "Stop looking so antsy," she said. "It will bring us unwanted attention. Act like you belong here, but use all your senses for situational observation." She sounded like her father. He wouldn't be pleased she had to use any of the training he'd drilled into her head. After all, the hope was she'd never have to use it, but he'd be happy that it'd helped her stay safe.

"Good point." Matt draped the jacket over the crook of his arm and lifted the phone to his ear. "We need police assistance. A cabdriver tried to abduct us and—"

Isabelle listened to Matt tell the dispatcher everything that'd just happened. Well, *almost* everything. Matt's calm, focused exterior likely meant the kiss hadn't fazed him one bit. He grabbed her hand with his free hand. It sent a shiver up her arm in a way his touch hadn't before.

"Yes, we're on Commercial. Headed to the pharmacy. I'll stay on." He looked to Isabelle. "Keep close."

"We're going back up there? What if they're driving around looking for us?"

His forehead creased in concern. "Cops are on the way to the pharmacy. It's just a block away. Besides, it's a one-way street, and we'll be going against traffic. I think we'll be safe."

She noticed he had the phone on speaker, which meant the dispatcher could hear everything she said. Isabelle pressed her lips together so she wouldn't object further. They began to climb the stairs up to the streets. Why did it feel like climbing to her doom?

Matt's insides were twisted tighter than a drawstring wrapped around a washing-machine agitator. Isabelle was right. He shouldn't look like a spooked horse, but trying to assess their surroundings using only his eyes made his heart ratchet up another notch.

He took comfort in the fact the dispatcher remained on the phone. Though realistically, what was she going to do if the men rounded the corner? Isabelle squeezed his hand tighter as they crested the final step. On top of the sidewalk, it seemed like a different world. This was the world of employees rushing home from a late work shift or meeting their coworkers for drinks. The streetlights weren't as bright as Matt would've liked, considering the situation.

"Matt," Isabelle whispered. "Nine o'clock."

For the briefest moment, Matt thought she was referring to the time. It had to be nearing ten o'clock by now. If they didn't hurry, the pharmacy would close. She elbowed him as they walked, and he turned his head to see. A man across the street looked at him but was walking on his own sidewalk. "What's the problem?"

"He's staring at us and matching our pace."

The man looked down at the ground and lengthened his stride. "See?" Matt said. "Nothing to worry about."

Only the man was crossing the street, and

his eyes had locked on them again. "What do we do?" he asked aloud.

"Sir?" The voice from the speaker rang out, jolting a few walkers headed in the opposite direction. "Your location?"

"Almost to the pharmacy. I can see the light at the corner. There's a man approaching."

"Sir, stay calm. Do you see a weapon?"

Matt lifted the phone to his ear so the stranger wouldn't hear. No need to put ideas in anyone's head. "No. Not yet."

Crack!

The bullet hit the trash can to the left of Matt. The man who had been crossing the street held his arms up and ran in the other direction. Isabelle didn't take the time to look behind them. She yanked Matt's arm and sprinted ahead.

He let her fingers slip through his hand as he pumped his arms to keep up with her. The bullet, just like last time, had been aimed at him. Whoever was after Isabelle wanted her to stay alive, which probably meant they still didn't have the laptop. And Matt was the only thing standing in their way.

He shoved Isabelle closer into the shadows as they passed the parking lot on the right. "Get down," Matt yelled.

Pedestrians screamed, though Matt couldn't see where the hollers were coming from. One street separated them from the pharmacy. Matt knew they had security protocols in place that would likely keep them safe if they could just get inside in time.

The crosswalk flipped to the red hand—cautioning pedestrians to stop. Isabelle didn't slow down. He strained to reach for the back of her shirt as he saw a silver car barreling down the street. "No!" The screech of the brakes hit his ears as his fingertips reached the back of her blouse.

Matt pulled, throwing his body backward. Isabelle screamed as she fell back into his chest. He fought against the momentum by twisting his torso, and they spun to the asphalt. He tightened every muscle he could as his arms tried to shield Isabelle.

Little bits of rock pressed into his shoulder, his triceps and his hip. Searing pain shot up his spine. The impact bounced his head off the sidewalk before he could stabilize his neck, but the bulk of his body had lessened the intensity. His temples throbbed, and his back begged for relief.

The driver's-side mirror shattered above him. He tucked his chin into Isabelle's back as the little pieces of glass sprinkled down around their feet. The gunman was still out there. Isabelle grunted and flipped over onto her hands and knees. She pressed her chin into her chest and began to crawl. "Come on. Get behind the car!"

His body screamed for him to stay, to take a rest. He ignored the pain and pressed up onto his hands and feet and ran low to the ground. As soon as they rounded the corner of the trunk, he reached underneath her torso and pulled her up to her feet so she could launch over the curb with him. They kept their heads low as they ran for the pharmacy, right at the corner. The automatic sliding glass door swished open without them having to slow down. "Lock it," Matt yelled.

The cashier looked wide-eyed but pressed a button and ran to fling down a lever that lowered bars across the windows.

Isabelle panted but pointed a shaking finger out the side window. "Wait. Look."

Two officers on bikes pulled up in front of the store. Matt looked to the left and to the right. The pedestrians had vanished. Not a single person was in sight. Even the driver of the silver car had driven off, no doubt terrified to stick around and get shot at some more.

The cashier released a shaky laugh and lifted the bars. One officer pointed at the door, and within a second the officers entered. "Was it something you said?" the cashier said with a smirk. "It's like a ghost town out there."

The officers ignored him and pointed at Matt. "Someone was shooting at you?"

Sirens filled the air as two police cruisers pulled up at the corner.

Matt looked down at his hand, expecting to see his smartphone still there. He groaned. Once the bullets started to fly, he'd lost track of it, most likely when they hit the deck. He really needed to start springing for the insurance. "Yes, from the east. I couldn't see where they were positioned, though."

One officer spoke in the radio clipped to his collar while the other officer gestured that everyone in the store move away from the windows. Matt turned to Isabelle. "Are you okay?"

"Thanks to you." She reached up to touch his forehead. "Oh, Matt. You're bleeding, and that's going to swell if we don't get some ice on it."

Her touch helped him forget about the rest of the pain. His fingers itched to pull her close and kiss her again. Never in his wildest dreams had he thought he'd be proposing marriage to Isabelle, even if it was pretend. But now it didn't seem like such a crazy idea. They might even be good together—if they could ever spend some time alone to find out without danger looming over their heads.

"Sir, do you need an ambulance?"

Matt waved the officer's question away, but the cashier pointed to the back of the store. "We have a first-aid kit with the pharmacist."

"That would be great. We also need to purchase some pepper spray. I heard you can get that over the counter?"

"I think so. You can direct your question to the pharmacist. Though I'm not sure pepper spray will do much good against bullets."

"That's what I'm worried about," Isabelle muttered.

"Humor me. It's better than nothing." Matt tried to smile through his own worry, but the truth was hard to avoid. Even if they were armed with all the self-defense tactics in the world, bullets always won.

TEN

Isabelle kept an eye on the officers from the back of the store. They seemed to be waiting for something. After the Tower situation, she wondered what it would take to get the police to agree to give her protection until the conference was over.

Matt followed her gaze and lowered the ice pack from his head. "I wish we knew who was targeting you. If we had an educated guess, maybe we could talk the DA into getting a court order for your protection."

She almost reached out to brush his hair back, to check on his injury. They were friends. Friends could do that…not usually after they'd pretended to get engaged, though. "Is that the only way to get police protection? A court order?"

Matt nodded. "I'm afraid so. Earlier today, an officer was making his rounds while I waited for you to finish the conference. I asked him about it. He said it makes the whole situation more difficult because we don't know who is targeting us."

She blew out a breath and pushed her hair back out of her face—the same hair that Matt had held back earlier. Her eyes drifted to his hands, and then his arms and the strong chest that had shielded her from hitting the ground at full force. He'd always been protective in high school, but she'd assumed it was in a big-brother sort of way. She never imagined he'd ever thought of her as anything more, even while her heart beat madly for him.

"The pharmacist says he's got a couple other orders he has to fill before he can get the pepper spray. Looks like we have time to kill."

She cringed at the innocent expression. It reminded her too much of the close calls. She turned away so she'd stop staring at him. "Do you ever think back on our friendship? About how odd it was?"

He shifted and stepped closer to her, which was the exact opposite of her intention. She felt his breath on her forehead.

"How do you mean?" he asked, his voice husky and soft.

"Don't you think it's rare that a guy and a girl would become best friends? I didn't think so at the time, but looking back—"

"Easy. We were a lot alike."

It was her turn to ask him what he meant, because from her vantage point, she couldn't grasp how he'd arrived at that conclusion.

"Don't get me wrong. We're still very different people," he said. "But we were both independent, both driven to succeed, both control freaks—"

"I'm flexible," she countered. "I moved all over the country. Home was wherever I was. And it's my out-of-the-box thinking that helped discover…" She caught the smirk on his face. "Okay, maybe I'm a little bit of both."

"You have to be. Just like I have to. It's what makes us good at the detail-oriented nature of our jobs."

"True." She tried her best to block out the words that ran through her head, the same words he claimed he'd only said because he was jealous all those years ago: *"intense, questioning everything, stubborn, logical to a fault, naive…"*

"Truth was, I didn't think of you as a girl back then," Matt said.

She felt her eyes bulge. "Excuse me?"

He held up his hands and smiled. "When you first moved in, you were someone new to hang out with…pure and simple. My brothers had gotten to the age that they were too cool to hang out with the youngest anymore." He pointed his thumb into his wide, strong chest.

She blinked hard, trying to focus on anything but how nice it had felt to be in his arms earlier. "So...I filled a vacancy?"

"Uh...no. Like I said, we're more alike than different. It was easy to hang out together. Only we put our energies into different things. I liked your friendship too much to let it matter once I realized you were a girl."

"You mean, once it *mattered* I was a girl."

He winked. "Semantics."

Another police officer walked through the glass doors, prompting a ding from the store speakers. They watched him converse with the other officers before he looked toward the pharmacy. He spotted Isabelle and approached.

"Ma'am, we've yet to find either of the two men you described. We're still combing the area and collecting witness statements."

"What about the man you caught the other night? The one you got outside the Tower of the Americas... Did you ask him for the names of the men? I'm sure they're all connected."

The officer put his hands on his hips. "I can't say much other than Jimmy Diaz—no confirmation yet as to whether that's his real name—proved not to be helpful." He looked at his shoes and sighed. "He was released on bail today."

Unaware she'd taken a step away, she felt her back press into Matt's solid chest. She didn't move forward. Frankly, she needed the support to remain standing. "So, he's still out there? Along with the others?"

"I'm afraid so." He shook his head. "They don't typically let officers know when they let these guys out. I found out only because of this shooting. I can assure you that your safety is a concern we don't take lightly. It's in our daily watch meetings. We will continue to increase patrolling around your hotel."

The rest of the questions and comments sounded like background noise. Matt took over the discussion, but she didn't pay any attention. Maybe she was wrong to have stayed this long. Her goal of fighting for a permanent home… maybe it was all selfish, all wrong. It'd certainly only brought Hank trouble and put Matt's life in danger.

"Isabelle."

She blinked and looked up to find Matt in her face, his head tilted in concern. "They've got the car waiting for us."

Perhaps this was what sleepwalking felt like—if she were ever aware of it—going through the motions in a dazed state of mind.

She approached the pharmacy counter to pick up the pepper spray that Matt had paid for. Except now Matt wasn't in sight. It served as another keen reminder that their ruse on the boat was all an act. After this, he probably wanted to stay as far away from her as possible, and she couldn't blame him.

Her shoulders bore the brunt of the stress as she forced herself to walk to the front of the store. Matt stood at the cash register. He winked and held up two phones. "To hold us over."

An hour ago she would've thought having a phone would've provided an added sense of security. Now it felt like she wasn't safe no matter what she did. Matt handed her the flip phone. "Were you listening when the officer asked you to call Hank?"

She inhaled sharply. "No. Why? Do they have some reason to think he's being targeted, too?"

"No, nothing like that." Matt placed a hand on her shoulder. "They need to know what number he called to order us the cab."

Her veins filled with icy liquid. "Are you implying—"

"If Sandra Parveen gave him a direct phone number, or he told someone else about it, then we might have a lead."

Her lips parted. While she was relieved he wasn't trying to insinuate her uncle was a suspect, it didn't make sense even to consider the conference organizer a suspect. Sandra wasn't an educated member in the field. She was an events coordinator, as evidenced by the way she hounded Matt for potential discounts. Uncle Hank, on the other hand, had already proved to have loose lips. "I'll call him as soon as possible."

The officer stood by the open back door of the police cruiser. If ever she'd wanted to feel like a criminal, now was her chance. And judging by the disapproving expression on the officer's face as he scanned the dark shadows around them, she might as well have been.

"At least we don't have handcuffs," Matt whispered. "If the gunmen weren't still out there somewhere, I'd ask him to drop us off a block from the hotel." Like a teenager trying not to be seen with his parents. Only this was much worse. It hadn't occurred to her until now that Matt's employees and guests would see him leaving the back of a police car. How humiliating. There wouldn't be any way around needing to explain that.

"Tell them everything, Matt. Don't let anyone think less of you because I got you into this situation. In fact, maybe I should make an announcement in the lobby when we get there."

"Stop." He laughed softly. "It's going to be okay, Isabelle. I appreciate the concern, though." He leaned over and squeezed her hand. Only she'd gone numb. She didn't want goals or dreams if they meant putting everyone she loved in jeopardy.

Isabelle flung herself back into the seat as if she'd been slapped.

Love. She loved Matt.

The cruiser pulled up in the semicircle drive underneath the hotel awning. Jake, Matt's valet, frowned but approached the car. When he caught sight of who was inside, his eyes widened.

Matt cringed. Maybe he should've taken Isabelle's offer a little more seriously.

The officer opened both of their doors for them. "Sir, is everything okay?" Jake asked. He looked over Matt's shoulder at Isabelle but said nothing.

"We avoided a close call."

Jake pursed his lips, his gaze on Matt's forehead. "Should've seen the other guy, right?"

Matt smirked, searching for a witty comeback. Isabelle joined him at his side. "The other guy had a gun."

Well, that took the humor out of the situation real fast. Jake paled. "Glad you're okay."

They walked through the glass front doors. Boisterous laughter to the right caught his attention. Mr. Frazer stood in the doorway of the small security office set off the entrance. He said something Matt couldn't decipher, and the guards inside burst into guffaws.

Matt approached, and Frazer spun around. "Matt, good to see you. Just shooting the breeze with your guards. Thought I went to school with Lyle here, but turns out he's just his funnier and smarter doppelgänger."

Lyle chuckled but didn't move from his spot in front of a screen with a plethora of hotel entrance angles on the monitors.

"You're back again, Mr. Frazer," Matt said.

Lyle jumped up and pointed to Matt's head. "Need the first-aid kit?"

Matt waved him away. He was trying to figure out the best way to handle the situation. He'd dealt with many unusual situations and unique people over the years, but he didn't like to act rashly. He needed to determine if the man really wanted to host an event or if he had other goals.

Frazer smiled amiably. "I was actually looking for you. I've been all over town today, and it seems you run the tightest ship. I think this might just be the place to have my daughter's wedding." Frazer held both hands up, but his gaze had moved to the monitor, which featured the police cruiser waiting in the driveway. "I'm not one to rush into things. I like to take my time and make sure of my investments." He sighed dramatically. "How about we start with a personal tour? I wanted to get my own impression before I received—no offense—your sales pitch. Now I'm ready for you to show me all the bells and whistles of this place."

An electric prickling sensation started at the back of Matt's neck. Usually he dealt with the wedding coordinator, the bride or the mother of the bride. Working with the father of the bride would be new territory. "Well, thank you. If you'd like to book an appointment to discuss possible—"

Isabelle's soft sigh eased his stress only a little. He'd forgotten she was behind him. She stepped back into the lobby, likely soothed that the situation didn't have anything to do with her. Matt leaned his aching back onto the side of the doorway. He crossed his arms and tilted his head. The man probably was old money and was used to doing things his way. Since the guy always showed up in the evenings, he was probably coming after business was done. He mentally ran through his own schedule. His family was due to arrive tomorrow night, but he should be able to squeeze in a mentor session of sorts. And if David happened to tag along so he could watch Matt at work, that'd be even better. "Why don't you stop by tomorrow evening? Same time?"

Frazer laughed. "Deal."

Matt tensed. Why, he couldn't quite pinpoint. "Well, it was nice to see you again." He stepped back onto the marbled lobby floor and saw Struther and Allen had flanked Isabelle. Were they staying here? He made a mental note to check the hotel roster before calling it a night. He wanted them both as far as possible from Isabelle. He didn't trust either one of them.

Concern flashed in her eyes at the sight of Matt. "They were across the street when they saw the police car pull out. They wanted to make sure I was okay."

"Will you still be able to present the keynote if they succeed in getting your laptop?" Struther asked.

"You don't think it could be someone from the conference, do you?" Allen raised both eyebrows.

Isabelle looked flustered by the questions delivered right on top of the other. Her right hand pressed into the area underneath her collarbone, just underneath the jeweled heart. "To be honest, the laptop isn't the biggest concern. I keep the research…elsewhere." She dropped her hand to her side.

Struther raised his eyebrows, his gaze fixed on her neck. "Smart," he commented.

She folded her arms across her chest. "And while I can't help but be cautious, I don't really think the danger is coming from within the conference. You both know that research like ours is often targeted by international organizations—"

"So true," Struther commented before she could finish. "You heard about West Coast Ocean Institute?"

"Of course," Isabelle said.

"Comes with the territory in our industry." Struther waved at Matt. "Well, glad to know you are okay. See you tomorrow, Isabelle."

Matt stared hard at both of them, unable to offer the slightest of smiles. Why would Struther—seemingly innocent of the Tower incident—not want to hear any more about the investment opportunity Isabelle could offer yet still be worried about her ability to present? They referenced West Coast Ocean Institute… He vaguely recalled Isabelle mentioning that they'd been hacked a month prior. And the two men seemed more like buddies now. Odd.

"Well, I'll see you around," Frazer said.

Matt spun around. "Uh, yes. Goodbye."

He led Isabelle back to his apartment so she could call Hank on his landline while their new phones charged. Every few steps, he took a glance over his shoulder to make sure no one was following them.

She cringed. "I'm sorry. After this week, I've likely turned you paranoid."

"Or more observant."

She grinned. "That's the positive way of looking at it."

He shrugged. "Now, *that* is your fault. Whereas I've likely made you take a more pessimistic view."

She stepped inside his place and dropped onto the couch. She leaned her head back and closed her eyes. "What a week."

The sight took him off guard—Isabelle comfortable in his home. His shoulders relaxed. It was as if she belonged here. And if danger and uncertainty weren't part of their lives, this week could've gone much differently. She'd changed, much as he had. But her essence, her gentle, caring heart, remained the same. She still loved the Lord, and her contagious smile still lit up a room.

Yet, even if the Lord answered his prayer in a heartbeat and made the danger nonexistent, there still wasn't hope for them to be anything more than friends. He sighed and turned away to open the phone packages on the counter in the kitchen. Ever since he'd known Isabelle, she'd wanted a place where she could grow roots.

Traveling had sounded fun to him, so he hadn't understood at first. Everywhere she went she could start over, get a new reputation and become whoever she wanted to be. Now that he'd moved a couple of times, he could see how it would get old fast.

Should Hank not be able to keep Isabelle on in her current position, she would likely need to move. Matt had no intention of staying put in San Antonio. He'd learned and worked his way to the top, but he could never implement all his ideas in a place where his boss worked from a city high-rise. It was all about the stocks and quarterly reports. His hope remained with his brother and sister-in-law, David and Aria. If they asked him to take over the conference center, then maybe he would have something to offer Isabelle, and he could consider pursuing her. Until then, he needed to control his thoughts...and feelings.

"Uncle Hank? Yes, we're fine. It's been quite a week." Isabelle's voice sounded strained from the other room. "I need to ask you a question.

Did someone give you the number to call a cab service for us?"

It wasn't lost on him that Isabelle didn't divulge the details of their night.

"She said what? Okay, one second."

Matt stepped into the room. Isabelle nodded at him, wide-eyed. "He said Mrs. Parveen mentioned that a lot of attendees claimed Grande Cab Service was the cheapest, but she didn't give him a phone number."

Matt nodded and went back to his phone, plugged in the outlet. It had enough battery power to make a phone call as long as it was plugged in. He pulled out the business card the officer at the pharmacy had given him before they'd left.

"Officer Taylor speaking."

Matt introduced himself and briefed him on what Hank had admitted.

The officer sighed. "I'm afraid that doesn't help us much. Grande really is the cheapest service in town. They're not known for the best service, though. Some reports have alleged organized crime has stemmed from the business, but we have no solid proof."

Matt raked a hand through his hair. "Wouldn't this constitute a lead?" He fought to keep emotion from entering his question. "I don't see any reason they would have an interest in Isabelle or her work."

"We'll look into it. Right now, the best thing you can do is stay in safe areas. Maybe use a different taxi service. We'll keep you updated."

He stared at the flip phone. Sometimes he missed being able to hang up by slamming the phone onto the cradle.

"Nothing?"

Matt spun around to Isabelle's soft voice. She still sat on the couch but leaned forward, her elbows on her knees and her face cradled in her hands. "They're looking into it," he said. He'd share what else the officer said as soon as he sat down. "How about I make some of my famous hot cocoa?"

"That'd be nice," she murmured.

The mugs with panoramic views of the River Walk seemed like the perfect choice since Isabelle wouldn't have the opportunity to enjoy the sights leisurely. A few moments later, he stepped toward the coffee table to find Isabelle asleep…and snoring softly. One hand was tucked underneath a throw pillow while the other was curled up beside her cheek.

If he woke her now, she might never go back to sleep. He'd certainly rest better in his room than in a wingback chair in the hallway. Especially since the gunmen seemed keen on killing him. He draped a blanket over her and made his way to his own room. If she tried to sleep-walk, he'd hear her. He was the lightest sleeper of his family.

He was too exhausted to change, so he kicked off his shoes, lay down on top of the covers and closed his eyes. Images of the gunmen and the car almost hitting Isabelle replayed in his mind on a loop. It seemed hard to believe that an organized crime ring would want anything to do with Isabelle's research.

His family would arrive tomorrow, and one thing was for certain—there was no way he could tell his mother. Because if she found out another one of her sons was a target of the mafia, there was no telling what she'd do.

ELEVEN

A stream of sunlight brushed against her face. Isabelle sighed and tried to roll, only to find her back against something firm. She bolted into a sitting position. Had she been sleepwalking again? The curtains looked familiar. A mug full of cold cocoa sat on the coffee table in front of her. Her ears strained and picked up Matt's deep breathing from the other room.

It meant that hours had passed without someone trying to kill them. She started breathing again, matching Matt's pattern of inhaling and exhaling, while her eyes and mind battled through the fog of heavy slumber. Surprisingly, she'd slept better than any other night she'd been in San Antonio, despite the hard couch.

Even though she never remembered dozing off, there must've been a part of her that trusted she could relax if Matt was there. Just like he'd been there the previous night, though he didn't realize she knew about his sacrifice. She had been getting ready to go back to bed when she'd heard a noise in the hallway. Through the peep-hole she'd spotted him, trying to get comfort-able in a stiff wingback chair right outside her door.

She smiled at the memory. It was one of the things she loved about him, his willingness to serve without glory.

There she went again, thinking she loved him.

The red LED clock on top of his desk blinked at her, as if scolding her for the thought. It flashed the time: 5:15 a.m. She could slip to her room, freshen up and get breakfast before the conference. Her stomach growled at the idea. She cringed at the noise and put her hands on her torso like she could mute it.

After she folded the blanket, slipped on her flats and found the cell phone he'd purchased for her, she crossed to open the door. Except she didn't want Matt to panic if he found her missing. On top of his desk, she wrote on a sticky note:

Don't worry. Not sleepwalking. I've got the phone. See you soon.

She placed it directly over the doorknob and unlatched the door. She inhaled and pressed the handle down, ever so gently, and slipped out into the hallway. The conversation with Hank last night weighed heavily on her mind. At what point did she admit defeat and cut her (and Hank's) losses? Such a break would force her to move again, and even though she hated the thought, it would free her up to a possibility with Matt.

Ridiculous. Matt hadn't shown any interest, and she'd practically opened the door for him to let her know if he did. But when she reflected on that kiss… Nope. Thinking about the kiss would now be off-limits. It meant nothing.

Isabelle sped through her shower and got dressed. She pulled the laptop out of the room safe. As far as she knew, the crooks after her still thought it resided in the main hotel safe. Matt had gone so far as to book her room under a pseudonym in case any crafty con man tricked the hotel staff into revealing her room number.

Oh, how she missed having a smartphone and tablet. The laptop had no network card, which meant no internet. To be without her email and productivity applications was a crime in and of itself.

She separated the flash drive from the rest of the necklace and plugged it into the computer. The presentation slides were in order and ready for her to practice. She whispered the words to herself. Tomorrow it would all be over.

Confident and prepared, she clicked off the slide show. Looking over her shoulder, despite the closed curtains and locked doors, she used the encryption to open the research files. If only she could entrust it to someone else or make it public. Then the danger would disappear…along with Hank's chance to pay the ever-increasing institute bills. So that wasn't an option. It wasn't as if she could walk away and the institute would continue to function. It'd be over and done, a huge vacuum in the community.

Her finger drifted over the facts and figures on the screen. Darren Allen would need assurances that she had cold hard data worthwhile to investors. She committed to memory as much as she could. The silence soothed her. She closed her eyes and prayed over the day.

Her room phone rang, jolting her. Should she answer?

"You nearly gave me a heart attack." Matt's voice was clipped.

"I left a note."

"I had to make sure it wasn't a sick prank. And then I couldn't help but wonder if you wrote the note in your sleep."

Coming from the king of pranks, it seemed

like poetic justice. It had taken two weeks for her mom to notice that Matt had slowly replaced all their framed family pictures with photos of Tom Selleck. Although, to be fair, her dad did have a slight resemblance.

"No prank. And I fully remember writing the note."

"Your first workshop starts in ninety minutes, right? I'll be down here with the catering truck and a to-go breakfast."

"Matt, you can't keep skipping work for me. Doesn't your family arrive today?"

"Don't worry about that. See you soon."

The same words she'd written on the note to him. Talking to someone in the morning, comparing schedules...it almost felt like she had a companion. Someone doing life with her, almost like a team ready to start a daily match. Maybe married life could be like—

Isabelle stood up, throwing the beginning of the thought to the side. She reassembled her flash-drive necklace, put the laptop back in the safe and took a deep breath. It seemed odd to count on Darren Allen, of all people, to help her get a deal today. If she succeeded, she'd soon place the research into the hands of a company with the funds to offer high-grade security.

Everything would go back to the way it was. Which meant getting back to life without Matt.

It shouldn't be that big a deal. She entered the elevator and pressed the Lobby button. She'd done life without him for years, happily and successfully. The silver doors opened. Matt shook hands with a couple about to head out the door, a smile on his face. She knew that look. He was good at his job. He'd found where he belonged. She imagined she had the same expression in the lab at home or when she took a group of schoolchildren on a tour of the tide pools.

Matt crossed the lobby to meet her. "How are you?"

"Amazing what a full night of sleep can do for a person."

"Well said." He waved her toward the side hallway. "We're going to shake it up and use the employee entrance, just in case our taxi friends are watching for us."

A small shiver ran up her spine. "Have you told your family about what's been happening?" She should've offered by now to change hotels. Her stomach twisted at the thought of being alone, though. The Lord was always with her—she knew that much—but she didn't want to do something foolish like making herself an easy target.

Matt cringed. "It didn't hit me until this morning that since they were trying to shoot me, that might put them in danger. I tried to call this morning, but they're already on a plane. They have a long layover in Los Angeles. I'll try them again, but I've already decided that a target on me justifies hiring more security. I'll be offering overtime shifts."

As soon as she got back home, she would begin saving to pay Matt back for his kindness. Even if the money didn't come out of his own pocket, she didn't want his generosity to make his actions unfavorable in corporate's eyes. Overtime had to run a pretty penny.

Matt turned to her. "One reason I moved up to the top so fast was my ability to streamline the operating expenses. We have enough reserve. So stop looking so guilty." He smirked as if proud of himself for guessing her thoughts.

She didn't want to admit that he knew her so well. She prided herself on being a woman of mystery, but it was hard to keep up that charade with Matt. The attempt to keep a straight face failed. "Okay. I'm glad."

"If they do come, my family is going to love seeing you again."

"Oh, please. As if they even will remember me."

He shook his head. "You'll see. Come on," he said. "Let's go save your institute."

"Oh, did the police find any leads on the cab thing?"

Matt tensed. "I actually got a call this morning. They found the cab that picked us up, but the company claimed someone had stolen it just minutes before."

She groaned. "So, another dead end?"

Matt hesitated.

"What is it?"

"The thing is, allegedly the business has ties to organized crime. There is a possibility that all those different guys who've been after you are part of—"

She gasped. "You've got to be kidding me. A mafia of sorts is going after my research? That seems nuts."

"Organized crime has one goal…profit. If someone wanted to hire their services, my guess is they'd consider it."

"In other words, we're no closer to finding out who is behind all this. What would they want with swarm intelligence?"

"I don't know. Isn't there a way you can skip all this and go straight to the Department of Defense for a grant? I mean, that would be the best option, right?"

"It doesn't work that way. Unless I grab their attention, we're relegated to waiting in a stack of unsolicited grant proposals. I'm not an engineer. I can't offer them proof it will benefit their programs. So, unless I wow somebody this week, it could take years to catch their notice."

"Ah." He sighed. "Now it all makes sense. I have no doubt you're going to get their attention when you give your presentation tomorrow."

She held up her index finger. "First of all, there is no guarantee a representative will even attend. I've heard rumors that one has popped in to a few of the workshops but that doesn't mean he'll come to mine. Second, you have no idea what my presentation is."

"Don't need to. I believe in you."

She dropped her hand. If only she believed in herself that much.

The entire day went by in a whirl. Matt insisted on being at the next table during her meeting with Darren Allen. If Darren asked, she'd say Matt was her bodyguard. That would be a rumor she actually hoped would spread... unless it put Matt in more danger.

It put her on edge that she had no one to trust inside the conference. Conventions such as this were supposed to bring people in the field closer together, but she'd experienced only the opposite thanks to the threat. Struther, Allen and even the conference organizer, Parveen, all gave her reason to be suspicious.

The meeting with Allen seemed more like a blip than the main event. She gave him the bare minimum of information, and he seemed to be excited. That almost worried her more.

"Let me talk to some of my people," he said. And that was it. She had no promises of when he'd get back to her, and he didn't want to reveal his contacts.

At five, Matt accompanied her back to the hotel, thanks to a ride from a former employee who was headed that direction after work anyway. She stepped out of the car as the man gave Matt a high five. "You seem to have a lot of former employees willing to give you favors. They were just that ecstatic to get away from you?"

"Can you blame them?"

"Very funny. No. Seriously, why do they like you so much?"

He gave a friendly wave at the security guard who, instead of sitting in the small office, stood guard right at the front of the entrance. She spotted another across the lobby, near one of the fire exits. "I try to find out what my employees' goals are and help them reach them, even if that means giving them stellar recommendations elsewhere."

Her mouth gaped. "That's unheard of. Don't you lose all your best employees?"

"On the contrary. Happy employees talk…

especially the former ones who often send high-quality applicants my way."

If she were the swooning type, that would've made her a bit wobbly. For her, having the thoughtful consideration to help employees reach their dreams ranked right up there with adopting rescue puppies.

They stepped into the elevator. She leaned against the back wall, soothed by the instrumental piano music piped into the speakers. It'd been a long day.

Matt's family was due to arrive soon. At least, he thought so. He'd mentioned leaving a bunch of messages without a response. They probably had their phones turned off during travel. But when they arrived, she didn't want to be in the way. She'd practically monopolized his time for the entire week.

Aside from avoiding feeling like a third wheel, she didn't want to get used to spending every moment with him. Loafing in sweats and enjoying some of that room service he'd offered sounded like the perfect evening. Matt stood next to the panel of buttons and pressed her floor number.

A well-dressed man caught the closing door. "Excuse me," he said. The man stepped inside. "Nine, please." She wondered what business he was in. His spine looked straight as a rod.

As Matt looked up at the illuminated floor numbers on the strip above him, the man, who'd also been watching silently, pulled a fist back and slammed it into the back of Matt's head so hard it bounced off the elevator wall.

Isabelle screamed and vaulted to the opposite corner of the elevator, cowering, as the man spun around to her. His eyes narrowed.

Matt flung an elbow backward into the attacker's back. The man stumbled forward. She jumped to the side, barely avoiding a collision. The guy's forehead hit the spot her head had been only a second prior.

Matt grabbed the red phone by the elevator panel and held it as if a weapon. "Stand down," he yelled.

The man growled as he spun and launched, fists out, toward Matt. Swiping the phone downward, Matt hit the man's left arm hard, though that didn't prevent his right fist from crashing into Matt's torso. Matt buckled over but managed to deflect the man's knee from connecting with his face.

Isabelle shoved her hand in her skirt pocket. Her fingers gripped the cold metallic canister of the spray they'd bought yesterday. She side-stepped their fight and pressed against the elevator doors, positioned to jump out as soon as the elevator stopped. If only she could reach the elevator panel, she would hit the next floor so this violent ride would end.

She kept her hand in her pocket as she flicked the safety valve of the pepper spray up with her thumb. She shoved her thumb underneath the valve, ready to depress it at the drop of a hat. They were pummeling each other with an intensity that made her insides shake. She wasn't sure she could get a direct shot if she tried. And if she missed, she'd set herself up for feeling the damaging effects of the spray in such a tiny, enclosed space.

The elevator dinged. The door slid open, and Isabelle stumbled backward into the hallway. "Stop it," she screamed at the man. He looked up, his eyes narrowing as if she was his new target. She withdrew the pepper spray out of her pocket and pressed the button in one smooth motion.

The stinging sensation instantly hit her nose as the stream of spray shot at least twenty feet, hitting the side of the man's face. It splashed off him, ricocheting all over the elevator as if someone had turned on the fire sprinklers. The assailant bellowed, retracting his fists to cover his own face. Matt also ducked his head, groaning.

With a sinking feeling, she realized she'd sprayed Matt, as well. "Help," Isabelle shrieked, hoping someone could hear her and would call the police.

The man let out a rage-filled war cry as he turned and lunged for her.

TWELVE

Matt kept his right eye open and reached out to grab the back of the man's shirt. His fingers brushed air. The burning sensation across his face, nose and eyes was so powerful he almost dropped to his knees.

The left side of his face felt like he'd flown too close to the sun while someone repeatedly bashed him with a cast-iron skillet. It went from severe sunburn to nuclear fission in two seconds flat. His left eye leaked so bad he couldn't bear even to squint out of it, and his sinuses acted as if he'd swallowed a blowtorch.

Through his right eye, he could make out the forms in front of him. Isabelle jumped to the side as the man ran directly into the opposite wall. He thundered and reared to charge again when the man spotted something and changed directions. He barreled past them both, sprinting toward the end of the hallway, perhaps toward the stairs.

Matt strained to care. He wanted the burning to stop. He wanted to shove his head into a shower.

Isabelle pounded on the next two doors. "Help!"

One of the doors was opened by a woman with a phone.

Isabelle rattled off instructions. "Call the police, please. And give me the milk from your minibar. I promise to reimburse you!"

The assailant stopped at the ice machine next to the stairwell and hit the button to get a bucketful, catching cubes with his hand. Matt forced himself to run after him. The breeze generated from running soothed his face slightly. The guy caught sight of him coming, though, shoved the ice against his face and disappeared through the stairwell.

"Matt!" A deep voice from the opposite end of the hallway caught his attention.

One of his guards was running toward him. "We have security waiting for him downstairs and police on the way."

"Good. Make sure to cover all the exits." Being still, even for a moment, caused the pain to thrust to the forefront of his mind.

Isabelle ran to him. "Lie down. Now." She held what looked like a plastic bottle of milk and a hotel washrag.

It was all he could do not to put his face underneath the ice machine. Instead he listened to her murmur words of encouragement as she poured the milk on his cheek, catching the streams with the rag. A moment later she draped the damp rag on his face. The milk began to soothe the pain. "I'm so sorry," she whispered.

He opened his right eye. "Pretty sure it's my own fault. I insisted you carry it. Bought myself my own punishment." Her face crumpled—compassion, worry and guilt written all over it. So, it probably wasn't the best time to tease. "You did the right thing, Isabelle."

"He's right, ma'am. Matt, they've got him in custody." The security guard held a walkie-talkie up to his mouth. "Watchman down. Caught in pepper spray. Please advise." He held up the speaker to his ear.

"Watchman?" Isabelle asked.

Matt cringed. "When I put through the order to beef up security, they insisted on using code names."

"Like the Secret Service?"

Matt took over holding the rag against his face so he could sit up. "Apparently the job can get boring." The pain still throbbed underneath his skin, but the milk made it bearable.

"The watchman," Isabelle repeated. "I like it."

"If you stuck around, they'd probably give you one."

"Willow," the security guard interjected. He shuffled his feet as if he spoke out of turn. "She seemed like a person of interest."

If he weren't in such pain, he'd have been amused.

The walkie-talkie squawked again. "Housekeeping is rushing up some baby shampoo, Matt. You're supposed to wash your face and eyes with it. Perhaps you could use her room? As soon as you're able, the police are waiting for you."

Matt just hoped that was all that was waiting for them.

Isabelle's nose and eyes stung, even though she hadn't suffered a direct hit from the spray. She refused to complain, though, especially standing next to Matt. He'd washed the affected area and said he felt much better, but the side of his face looked as if he'd been attacked by five-year-olds armed with blush. He really needed to change his clothes, as well, or she might never stop sneezing. His jacket reeked.

The housekeeping crew was cleaning the elevator. They wore masks as they mopped and wiped down all the surfaces. Isabelle gave them an apologetic wave as they waited for the other elevator. Thankfully the security guard rode down with them. Otherwise Isabelle wasn't sure she could handle stepping into a moving box again.

As they entered the marbled lobby, she wouldn't have even known something criminal had occurred. The soothing piano ballads played through the speakers, and some guests of the hotel mingled around the couches and lounge chairs. One of the hotel employees waved Matt toward the registration. "You have some *people* waiting in your office."

She followed Matt into a side door marked Employees Only. A police officer was speaking to Lyle, the security guard who seemed to be in charge. The officer turned to them. "I have good news and bad news. You mentioned a car was shot near the pharmacy yesterday. Late last night, the driver came forward. He'd allegedly spotted the gunman while driving away. The man we just arrested matches the description of the shooter."

Isabelle blew out a breath. She wasn't sure she wanted to know the rest. "And the bad news?"

"He's using the same lawyer as Jimmy Diaz."

Her pulse quickened. "Doesn't that count as evidence that they're conspiring, or colluding, or whatever legal term you want to use?"

"That's not how it works, ma'am."

"So he'll likely be released on bail soon," Matt said. "Even though you suspect they're part of the mafia."

The officer raised his eyebrows. "There may be rumors, but I can't officially confirm any of them. I am afraid the likelihood of bail is high. We're keeping an eye on Diaz, so if this guy gets out, we'll do the same, but I won't pretend the danger isn't there. Can you offer us anything on what they may be after that can help us pinpoint their motivation?"

In other words, was there any way she could tie all these seemingly random attacks to an unnamed organized crime ring? It was ludicrous. If the instigator was someone in the industry, she could buy that. Organized crime usually focused on drugs and extortion and...well, she didn't really know, but they didn't have the reputation of stealing academic research. She sighed. "I have research they're after. Tomorrow I'll be presenting on it—'Particle Swarm Optimization, Velocity Redefinition and Mutation Factors for Permutation Solutions.'"

The officer stared at her for a moment. "I'm afraid that doesn't give us much to go on."

She threw her hands out. "Well, that's all I have. They've taken everything else I own."

He shook his head as if trying to think of

something. "We'll do our best to find something, but aside from what we're already doing, you might want to consider hiring a bodyguard. If that's not possible, I suggest asking the conference center and hotel to hire extra security. We'll continue to patrol the area around the hotel and the conference center." He nodded at her. "Call us if you think of anything else." The officer made a circular gesture toward Matt's face. "Stings, doesn't it?" He let himself out of the office and headed out the door.

"Fat lot of good that did," she muttered.

Matt glanced at the clock on the wall, and his eyes widened. "My family will be here soon." He stormed out of the office.

Now would be a good time to offer to move to a different hotel, but she hadn't called Hank yet. She followed him out.

Mr. Frazer stood waiting for him. Matt placed a hand on his forehead, which she almost pointed out wasn't a good idea. He shouldn't touch his face at all until he'd changed clothes and was sure all the pepper-spray oils were gone. Otherwise he'd spread it further, but she didn't want to embarrass him in front of his coworkers.

"Mr. Frazer, I'm terribly sorry," Matt said. "I thought I could squeeze you in today, but something has come up." Matt turned to the registration desk. "Is the Ambassador Suite ready for my family?"

"Absolutely. Checked myself," Ellen answered.

"Perfect. Could you have a bellhop—I don't know who's on duty tonight—grab Miss Barrows's things and take them to the suite?"

Isabelle took a step forward. "What? I can't stay with your family."

"Of course you can. There's plenty of room. And, Ellen, would you ring Rosa and ask her to give Mr. Frazer a tour? She should almost be done with the Townsend rehearsal."

Matt reached over the side of the counter for a pad of paper. He tore off the top sheet and handed it to Mr. Frazer. "Rosa is my right hand."

Frazer shook his head. "Well, I was really hoping for you. You're supposed to be the best."

"And I appreciate that, but unless you can wait until next week, I can't make it work."

Frazer narrowed his eyes. "I'll wait for Rosa."

Matt nodded, said his goodbyes and darted down the hallway to change while Lyle guarded Isabelle like a hawk. The way he stepped in front of her, his shoulders back and his eyes scanning the room, she knew he took his job seriously. "You like working here?"

He nodded without looking at her. "A whole lot better since Matt became my boss. You've got a good man there."

Her cheeks heated. "He's not exactly mine, but I agree he's a good man."

"Well, you better make him yours. About time he stopped working so hard and learned to enjoy the fruit of his labors." Lyle said it with such severity she almost snickered.

It was obvious Matt shared the same work ethic she did. Every time she watched him in action, her heart beat a little faster. There was something attractive about a person who'd found what he was really good at and yet still strived for excellence.

Matt strode across the lobby before she could reflect further. His face had almost turned back to its normal color. "Ready?" He gestured at the elevators. "I'm starting to hate these metal boxes."

"But better than stairs, right?"

"Absolutely." The pepper smell had been replaced with the cedar smells she enjoyed.

He pressed the button for the thirtieth floor. As the doors began to close, he took a giant step backward, no doubt to give himself a better vantage point should anyone enter at the last second.

She grabbed Matt's arm, instantly regretting

it because of the heat that traveled up her arm when he looked at her in surprise. "I…uh…realized I have to stop by the room. My laptop is still in the room safe. The bellhop can't access it without the code, can he?"

"I should've remembered. No, he can't. Let's see if he has already dropped off your stuff, and then I can run down and get it while you are settled. Though you'd have to trust me with the code. I mean, I understand if—"

"I do." The words slipped out of her mouth before she realized what they sounded like… the affirmation of wedding vows. Her mind kept going there. What was wrong with her? It never had done that with any other man she'd ever dated.

And sure, should the unthinkable happen and Hank needed to close the institute, she could get a job in San Antonio. If she had to, she'd give tours at SeaWorld until she could find an opening in research. Maybe San Antonio could be her forever home…if Matt felt the same way she did. But that was a giant if.

She inhaled, taking control of her thoughts. "I can't imagine you'd ever want to leave here. Your employees would clearly do anything for you. They're a genuine team. That's rare, you know."

"Thank you." His chest seemed to puff a bit. "But I'm not staying."

"What?"

"I've come to realize this week that my staff could run this place without me." He gave her a side glance. "I have you to thank for that. I haven't allowed myself any time off to give them a chance to show me."

"But th-that's the mark of a good manager! You've trained them well. But they'll still need you if there is a hiccup. I'm sure there is a ton of other things they couldn't do without—"

"You're right, but I'm not ready to settle down until I find somewhere to implement my own ideas and vision." He shrugged. "If that place isn't with David's venture, then I'll keep looking until I find it. One day I hope to have built enough clout that I won't be seen as a risk. I just need someone to believe in me."

She slumped up against the side of the elevator. "I believe in you."

Of course his dream would be the exact opposite of hers. That was the way the world seemed to work, in her experience. Though, if she were honest, part of *her* dream included a family. If she had the opportunity to marry and start a family with her best friend, would she say no because it meant moving a lot? It was something she had vowed she'd never do.

It was enough to turn Randy down, but her heart had never been fully invested in that relationship. What'd her mom always say? *Home is where the heart is.* It sounded like a platitude more than a quote from Pliny, a Roman philosopher two thousand years ago. Either way, she'd disregarded the sentiment. But maybe it was worth revisiting. Was she merely trying to justify the possibility of walking away from her dream?

That philosopher had one thing right, though, when he said, "No mortal man moreover is wise at all moments." The stress of the unknown, the danger of the week, and her heart's longing to stay connected with Matt. It was all becoming too much to bear. She needed wisdom.

A verse in James basically said if someone lacked wisdom, she should ask God, who gives it generously without fault. *I'm asking, Lord.*

"I appreciate that more than you know," Matt said.

Isabelle blinked and wondered if she'd prayed aloud until she realized he was responding to her comment about believing in him. "I'm sure your employees and family would agree with me," she said.

"I hope so. If I ever reach the point that I'm doing it just for the money and recognition, then I think I'll need to move on to a different career. 'Where your treasure is, there your heart be also.' Right?" The doors swung open and he stepped into the hallway.

Isabelle didn't move. "What did you say?"

He frowned and pressed a hand to keep the doors open. "'Where your treasure is, there your heart be also.' It's a verse."

"I—I know." The words hit her in a way they never had before. She would have to digest the timing of him quoting that verse a little later. Sure, it was figurative, but maybe she should consider taking it for the literal meaning, as well. She certainly treasured her relationship with Matt. She sighed and stepped out to join him.

Matt pulled out a hotel key and stuck it in the closest hotel door. "I figure it must be important because it's quoted twice, in Matthew and in Luke."

Way to make a point, Lord. Her gaze flickered upward. *But I don't want to jump to conclusions, so excuse me if I'm being thickheaded. I really need it to be crystal clear.*

The door swung open. "After you." She followed Matt's hand and stepped inside. Despite the darkness, her focus swept past the room to the windows. The first set of doors opened to a balcony. The other two sets of windows took up most of the wall space. In front of her was a wonderful view of the San Antonio skyline. It was a luxury to enjoy the view without needing to network with other people or watch it speed by in an elevator.

Matt kept his gaze down. "Go ahead. Take a look. I'm going to make sure everything is ready for my family."

Isabelle strolled past a dining-room table and a set of couches on her way to the balcony. In the middle of the table, a large basket was filled with San Antonio souvenirs. Matt really left no detail undone. His family would be impressed.

She put a hand on each of the door levers, pushed down and swung the French doors open at the same time. The refreshing air blew her hair back, the closest she would get to the sensation of flying. This high up, despite the city lights, she felt she could almost touch the sky.

A hand grabbed her shoulder. She turned, surprised Matt would join her with his fear of heights. But it wasn't his eyes she stared into.

Her smile dropped. The man with the knife who had chased her into the grotto faced her.

Her mouth wrenched open to scream, but the man shoved a gloved hand over her face. She fought to breathe.

She shoved him with both fists, but he didn't budge. She pulled her leg back to kick him, but he propelled her backward until the small of her back pressed against something metal. The rest of her torso felt the wind rushing past. Cold dread spiked her heart rate as she flung her head side to side, trying to free herself of his grasp, desperate for a deep breath.

"That'll be all." His cold hard voice met her ears at the same time his hand loosened around her face and dropped to her neck. She inhaled a greedy breath. He shoved his right hand into her chest as he yanked on the necklace with his left. The chain bit into the back of her neck. She cried out until it mercifully broke free, leaving a stinging, hot, liquid sensation.

He shoved her. Her back threatened to snap as her torso bent. Her hands reached out to find nothing but air as he flipped her the rest of the way over the balcony.

THIRTEEN

Matt flipped on the lights of the full kitchen. So far everything looked in perfect order. He was pleased all the curtains had remained closed in every room but the entrance. He wanted his family to enjoy the aha moment of the beautiful city, but there was only so much he could take of the views before the slow build of fear made him nauseated.

A doctor told him the medical term was "acrophobia." It'd been something he'd prayed about for as long as he could remember, especially since he'd grown up desperate to follow in his father's footsteps. Essentially he didn't trust his own sense of balance when faced with heights. As long as he didn't have to climb a ladder or stand near a balcony or cliff, he was able to cope. He could even fly in an airplane as long as he kept his gaze forward.

A noise shook him out of his thoughts. Perhaps the door. Maybe the bellhop had arrived to deliver Isabelle's things. The two-thousand-square-foot suite was about as spread out as a one-story house. He turned each set of lights off as he walked back toward the entry. "Isabelle?" he called out.

He stepped into the living room and averted his gaze from the window. "Isabelle?"

Something slammed into his side. He crashed over the side table and smashed into the wall, his shoulder taking much of the brunt force. A dark shadow wrenched open the front door and disappeared into the hallway.

Matt jumped up. The man had come from…

The realization took his breath away. A breeze blew in from the open balcony doors, carrying only the sounds of traffic in the streets below. "Isabelle?" His blood pressure spiked, and his temples throbbed. "Isabelle!"

He forced himself to run to the balcony. A whimper brought him to his knees. He couldn't see her, but he could hear her gasping for air. "Where are you?"

"Uh—under." Her voice sounded panicked, high-pitched.

Matt gulped and forced his forehead against the metal bars. He still couldn't see her, but he could see the distance to the cement below. His stomach turned and he gritted his teeth. "Hang on. I need to call for help."

"I'm slipping, Matt! I can't!"

The terror in her voice vaulted him to standing. *Lord, help.* He gripped the top of the balcony and blew out a breath as he bent over the balcony. His stomach threatened to lose the remains of his lunch.

Underneath the edge of the balcony, Isabelle clung to the metallic decorative trim. Her wide eyes met his. Her chest rose and fell rapidly. Why'd he have to get the fanciest suite on the top floor? If he'd just picked one of the normal rooms, she'd have had a balcony below she might've been able to get to. He wasn't good at guessing distances, but at this point she'd drop fifty to a hundred feet onto the pavement surrounding the terrace pool on the twentieth floor.

Even if he bent over as far as possible, he wouldn't be able to reach her without falling himself. Matt gauged her position. He squatted down and stuck his arm through the metal railing until his shoulder prevented it from going any farther. He couldn't see her but knew his hand had to be close. "Grab my wrist!"

"I don't think I can let go," she cried.

"One hand. Come on—you can do it. You can do anything when you set your mind to it." He knew that for a fact, especially when she got angry. "Come on, Izzy," he taunted. "You never did the monkey bars before? Leave one hand on the metal and grab me."

She grunted. "I told you. Don't—" she took a breath "—call—" a hand latched on to his wrist "—me Izzy."

Her weight pulled down his arm in an unnatural position, tightly wedged between the metal bars. He worried for a half second whether he'd just made things worse. He closed his eyes and mentally constructed a game plan. But if he made one wrong move, she'd fall to her death.

He breathed out and twisted his hand so his own fingers could latch on to her forearm. No easy feat without being able to see her. "Don't let go."

"Same to you," she screamed back.

"Okay, okay," he said, mostly to himself. "We need to take this one step at a time. What if— What about I try to swing you toward the pool?"

"Don't you dare!" Her voice rose an octave. "It's not happening. Margin of error is too big, and I'm not letting you go."

"Fair enough." He inhaled through his nose. His knees couldn't handle squatting much longer. "You still have one hand on that bar, right? I'm going to need you to put both hands on my arm if I'm going to get you back up here."

She let out another guttural scream and the

fingertips from her other hand dug into his arm. He flinched but tried to keep his grip on the one forearm. "Nails!" His right arm felt like it was about to dislocate itself. He took a big inhalation and pressed his heels into the ground as he stretched his left side to reach the top of the balcony with his other hand. His palm and fingers wrapped around the sharp edges.

"Matt…" Her breathing was rapid. His arm bounced painfully against the metal bars. Isabelle had to be flailing and taking his arm with her.

"Try to stay still."

"I can't. There's nothing underneath me!"

"Okay. Here we go. It's going to be fine." He took three big breaths. Then, with every ounce of strength, he pressed into his heels. It was like a weird combination of a deadlift squat and a shoulder raise with over one hundred pounds. The tendons in his neck felt like they were about to rip from the strain. He pulled as much with his left arm as he pushed with his legs.

Inch by inch he lifted her as he pulled his arm back through the bars. Her face came into view. Tears glistened from the moonlight. A gust of wind blew her hair into a frenzy. He tightened his grip.

"Ow," she cried.

"Sorry, sorry. Almost there." He stood in an awkward diagonal bend. He couldn't lift her any more from this vantage point. "Okay, you should be able to grab the bottom of the bars in front of you."

"I can't let go!" Her legs began to flail some more.

Matt's heart pumped so hard he could hear it in his ears. "Put one hand on a bar. Just one hand."

Her wide eyes met his for the briefest of seconds. The thought of losing her scared him more than dropping to his own demise. He wouldn't let her fall. He couldn't. His heart would self-destruct. She screamed as she let go and grabbed the nearest bar. *Please let someone hear her scream and help.*

"Okay, okay." He hoped his voice would help keep her calm. He needed to think. It was just a puzzle that needed to be solved. He shoved the tips of his shoes as far underneath the space between the balcony bars and the balcony floor as he could. *Please let these bolts hold, Lord, because I'm about to throw all my weight on these bars.* If the bars went, they both went.

He made the mistake of looking down, and he gagged. Oh, no. No. He couldn't afford to have this fear now. He needed to focus and keep his mind on the task, and the girl, at hand.

His left hand released the top bar. The stinging sensation from having wrapped his palm around the sharp edges barely registered. He leaned forward until his left hand was hanging down over the balcony as far as he could get it. "Grab my left hand." His toes strained against the entire balcony. A creak of metal sounded behind him.

"What was that?" she screeched.

A reminder he needed to work fast. His left arm bore the punishment of her flailing. "Good. Now your other hand needs to let go of the bar. Grab my right hand."

She shot him an exasperated stare.

"I'm sorry, honey. I'm trying my best."

"Just don't give up," she said with a pant.

"Hello?" a familiar male voice called. "Matt? Matt! Don't do it!"

A moment later, over shouts of exclamation, arms and hands joined his effort. He stayed focused, Isabelle's eyes locked on his. Someone grabbed his torso for stability while other arms reached down and grabbed Isabelle's wrists. In the back of his mind he knew his family had arrived, but he couldn't speak, couldn't process.

"One, two, three." Everyone tugged upward until Isabelle's feet touched the outside of the balcony bars.

One hand moved upward and grabbed his neck. "Don't let go," Isabelle cried.

He wrapped one arm around her waist, and his brothers helped pull her up and over until she was fully and completely in his arms, leaning into his chest. His brothers stared at him slack-jawed.

"What was that?" his mom yelled, smacking him on the shoulder. "You almost gave your father a heart attack."

"I'm fine," his dad muttered.

"Call the police, Mom. A man attacked us. He pushed her over." A knock sounded as his new hire Ben, the bellhop, entered. "Call security, Ben."

He bent down to look at Isabelle. Her eyes were closed tight and her arms wrapped around his neck. His brother David led him to the closest couch. "You're safe now," he said. "Do you need an ambulance?"

Matt sat down. She looked out of one eye, then finally opened both. The grip on his neck loosened. She moved to sit on her own couch cushion, but her entire body was shaking like a leaf. He kept his arm around her shoulders, pulling her close to stop the shivering.

James rushed over with a golden microfiber blanket. "She needs something warm before she goes into shock. An ambulance might not be a bad idea."

"Police are on their way. What is going on?" his mom demanded.

"It's a long story, Ma."

"At least we know you've outgrown your fear of heights. I always knew you would," his dad said proudly.

Matt couldn't form enough words to respond to his dad at the moment.

His forearm felt a wet heat. He pulled his arm back and looked at Isabelle. "You're bleeding."

She pulled away from Matt and blinked, taking in the crowd of the room. All the voices and questions began to seep into her conscience. "Uh…no, I don't need an ambulance. I'm not in medical shock. Emotional maybe."

Her blood pounded hard against her wrists. The stinging returned at the back of her neck. She pulled the back of her hair up and looked at Matt. The roller coaster of being thankful to be alive coupled with the defeat of losing her research was almost too much to process. "They got it. They took the flash drive." She reached tentative fingers to where the chain used to be. "Is it bleeding badly?"

"I'll tell security to bring up a first-aid kit,"

James said. He hopped up from his knees and strode to the phone.

"Isabelle?" Luke asked. "Is that you?"

"Why, it is," Matt's mom gushed. "Oh, Isabelle." His mom rushed over to hug her. "I always hoped you and Matt would find each other again."

Matt leaned back into the cushion. "You did?"

The incredulous disbelief reverberated off his words. As if he could never in his lifetime imagine them together. Great. The night couldn't possibly get any worse. "Hello, Mrs. McGuire. Everyone," she added, nodding a greeting to the three brothers and Mr. McGuire. They stood in a semicircle around her. "I'm surprised you remember me."

Luke smirked. "No one forgets a girl who invites herself over at three a.m. for a sandwich."

"And chips," David added.

"Don't forget she wanted to watch James Bond," James interjected with the phone pressed to his ear.

Matt's dad chuckled. "Hello Kitty pajamas and pigtail braids."

Heat flushed her cheeks. Okay, the night could get worse. It made her sound more like she'd been a third grader than a teenager. The braids had been useful to tame her wild curls.

Thankfully there were products she could buy that could help now.

His dad coughed away the laugh. "And of course, you were my right hand for a couple summers. Couldn't forget that."

"Where's the rest of the family?" Matt asked, ignoring their jabs at her. "I don't want them wandering around when that man might still be in the building."

Everyone sobered.

Mrs. McGuire pulled out her cell phone and began dialing. "The girls went to check out the spa services. The twins are with them."

"James, tell security to escort them up here," Matt said, talking over James as he requested the first-aid kit. James nodded to indicate he'd heard.

The girls? The twins? Isabelle frowned, trying to remember if Matt had mentioned them. Matt must have spotted her confusion because he added, "Aria is David's wife. Gabriella is Luke's wife, and James has twin boys. He's newly married to Rachel."

So, everyone had gotten married but Matt? Did that make him feel as out of place as not being involved in David's business did?

"I want to know what's going on," Mrs. McGuire said. "Is that what all those messages were about?"

"So, you did get them," Matt said. "Why didn't you call me back? I really didn't want to put you guys in a position of potential danger."

"You said there was a situation, not a man trying to kill you," his mom replied.

"It's not something I wanted to leave by voice mail. I thought you would call me back."

"And I thought you were just busy with work. I didn't want you to try to talk us out of a visit. And even if I had known, I still would've come. I just might have sent the rest of the family home." She pulled her shoulders back. "What's done is done. Tell me what's happening so we can decide how to move forward."

While Matt's mother wasn't actively a police detective, she still questioned him like she was. Matt explained the situation. He fumbled over describing Isabelle's research, but she didn't correct him. It didn't matter. It was gone. Whoever had been responsible for the week of terror had succeeded. But they also seemed to want her dead. She had no idea if they would stop going after her now that they had the research. And did they have the technology capable of breaking the encryption?

"What about the laptop you mentioned?" James interjected.

"It's still in the room safe," Isabelle answered.

He scratched his head. "So you have a copy of the research there."

"No. It only runs modeling software and the encryption key."

James grinned. "For the flash drive? So that means they might not be able to access your research yet."

She clasped her hands together. "That was the hope, but the last guy who held us at gunpoint seemed pretty confident they'd already accounted for breaking through the security."

"What'd you use?"

She explained the hardware-based encryption she used as well as the ciphers. James nodded appreciatively. "And you ended up with my brother?"

Matt's eyes widened, but he didn't say anything.

"No, we're just friends," Isabelle answered.

The bellhop opened the door to let in the security team, the police, a group of women and children—presumably all from the McGuire clan—and two racks of luggage, one of which held her carry-on bag.

The police assured them they were still following up on other leads. Isabelle just wanted to be done and get home to Oregon. There didn't seem to be any point in staying. Maybe she could ride standby and get home faster. Although she had no guarantee it would still be her home if she were out of a job.

The wives of Matt's brothers all smiled and introduced themselves. She didn't exactly feel like talking. Instead she stared at the floor because she couldn't bear to look them in the eyes any longer. She was the one ruining their family vacation and the reason they couldn't wander around.

Once the police left, Matt posted a security guard outside their room. "I think we need to get that laptop," James said.

"I do need it back eventually," Isabelle said. "But only to return to my boss. There's no rush. It's no longer that valuable."

James held up a finger. "Don't give up so soon. Matt mentioned they were after the laptop in the beginning. But something switched their focus, so they went after the flash drive."

Matt jumped to standing. "Struther. You were holding the flash drive when you were talking to him and Allen. You didn't say that's where you were keeping it, but it did seem to capture his attention."

She pulled her arms in close. In other words, she'd messed up yet again.

"I knew I didn't trust those guys," Matt spewed.

"Okay," James said, "but they'll realize soon they need the laptop, as well."

"I've heard enough!" Mrs. McGuire stormed over to the stack of luggage near the door. She unlocked a small hard case and pulled out a gun.

"Whoa! Mom!" Matt had his hands up. "How on earth did you bring that on a plane?"

"Don't look so surprised. I checked it, followed procedure." She pulled out a stretchy piece of black fabric and wrapped it around her hips. The gun and a clip of ammo slipped inside unseen pockets before she pulled her shirt down over it. "It's not as if I didn't carry when I worked as a police detective. A fact that all of you apparently have forgotten or you would've called me the minute this all started."

David frowned. "Since when did you start carrying again?"

"Since you boys keep getting yourselves in trouble, that's when."

Aria cringed. "I think that was actually more my fault than his."

"Ditto," Gabriella interjected.

Rachel shook her head. "Not me. That was all him." She pointed at James but had a smile on her face. The loving way each daughter-in-law gazed at her man reminded Isabelle she was an outsider.

She turned to look away but found Matt staring back at her. Oh, he was waiting for her to stick up for him. "It was my fault, Mrs. McGuire. Obviously."

"Your mother's been hitting target practice while I golf," Mr. McGuire said. "So if you need to give that security guard of yours a break, Matt, your mother is still as sharp as ever."

"Maybe you should accompany them to get her laptop," James said. "Because if I had a chance to finish a sentence around here, I was going to let you know I could set up a honey pot."

She'd heard of those before. "To lure them to a fake software key? Except that won't work. The laptop doesn't have a network card. They can't access it online."

He smiled. "Good. That was smart. But do they know that?"

She pursed her lips and tried to replay every word she'd said regarding the laptop in the past week. Tension slowly left her back. "No. I'm sure I didn't tell anyone but Matt."

"So I can install a network card easily. When were you supposed to present your research?"

"Tomorrow. It won't be as impressive without the numbers and my slide show, but I can say enough from memory that I think it'll still be interesting."

James nodded. "That gives me enough time

to set up the lure. If they haven't succeeded in hacking the encryption by then, they will be getting desperate."

"Which means they'll go after Isabelle again." Matt's mouth formed a grim line.

"You have no guarantee that they won't anyway," James replied. "But if I set up a honey pot on her computer, I'll be able to track them."

Hope sparked. Isabelle leaned forward. "You could really do that?"

Luke smirked. "James used to work for No Such Agency."

The other brothers laughed, but Isabelle was slow to catch on.

Rachel rolled her eyes. "He means the National Security Agency."

"Oh. Wow." If James had that kind of experience, maybe things weren't as grim as she'd thought. "Well, that sounds like a doable plan to me."

Matt shook his head. "No way. That's almost like setting yourself up as bait."

His mom put a hand on his shoulder. "No. Because we'd coordinate our efforts with the police, honey. I have a good idea of their procedures. We can work alongside to make sure she has backup. If the police are on board, it sounds like a good chance to get these attackers behind bars. And you and Isabelle will be safe once and for all."

"It's too much to ask of all of you," Isabelle said.

Mr. McGuire waved her concern away.

Matt closed his eyes and sucked in a deep breath. His eyes flashed open, and he stared at Isabelle so hard she almost asked aloud what he could be thinking. "If...if you're okay with this," he finally said, "then I guess we've got ourselves a plan."

She tried to smile, but her burning eyes only welled up with tears. Because one thing was certain: ever since she stepped off that plane, none of her plans had succeeded.

FOURTEEN

Matt couldn't believe what he was hearing. "Are you sure?"

The police officer nodded. "None of your security cameras picked up the man you and Miss Barrows described as attacking you."

His breath turned so hot he wouldn't have been surprised if he started breathing fire. Not only did they have no leads on Isabelle's attacker, but also his whole family got a front-row seat to hearing his security system was subpar.

"Grant me permission to check your system," James whispered behind him.

Matt whirled around. "What do you think you're going to find?"

James shrugged. "I'm pretty good at finding a glitch in systems."

"It's just cameras."

"That can be hacked," Isabelle said. She'd been listening.

"Fine. Go."

"I wish I had more to tell you," the officer said.

"Thank you for your time," Mom replied.

"We'll be keeping a car close to the vicinity. Don't hesitate to call." The officer placed the hat back on his head and exited the suite.

For the rest of the night Matt barely heard the conversations going on around him. His sisters-in-law chose a restaurant and called in a delivery order. James confirmed that the security system had, in fact, been hacked by professionals.

Matt didn't have a response. They'd been outmaneuvered and outfoxed every step of the way. If giving up hadn't meant lives on the line, he'd have considered waving a white flag.

Even his sweet nephews couldn't shake him out of the fog. And if Isabelle asked him one more time if he was okay, he would snap. She drew closer to other people when stressed, whereas Matt just needed time alone to process. Something he couldn't do with his entire family staying in the hotel that was meant to impress them, instead of appearing to be a death trap.

Isabelle sat next to James at the dining-room table, pointing to her laptop. Matt's concierge had sent out for a network card that James would install the next morning, when the honey pot would be live. Apparently the honey pot would consist of data that would look almost identical to the real security encryption key Isabelle used. But instead of unlocking her flash drive, it would track down whoever was trying to do so.

As soon as her computer went online, theoretically, any hackers in the area would be able to see her computer identity, which James also made sure was veiled—but barely. He had to make it difficult so it wasn't obvious as a trap, but not too difficult. "I have a pretty good idea of their skill level based on what I saw on the security system," James said.

Rachel and Gabriella boxed up the leftovers from their Casa Rio takeout. Isabelle smiled at them. "Thank you all for letting me be a part of your family reunion tonight. As long as tomorrow goes smoothly, I'll be on a flight out by that night. Ideally I'll take the drama with me."

In other words, she'd be out of his life again. It left a hollow feeling in his rib cage. And by drama, she meant danger. The last thing he wanted was for her to take the threat with her. He would bear the signs of her fingernails hanging from his arms for a few days, but he didn't need the reminder. The image of her terrified wide eyes was burned into his memory. It'd be impossible to forget that he'd almost lost her. The helpless feeling punched him in the stomach, and it was almost enough to make him scream in frustration.

"Give Uncle Matt a hug," James said. "I think he needs it."

Matt barely registered the words before the twin preschoolers launched in the air and landed in his lap. He dived forward, his arms circling around each of them as he fake-wrestled them to the ground. Luke growled and joined him in the pretend dog pile, extremely careful not to put any real pressure on the giggling boys.

David and James didn't disappoint, joining in.

"So much for getting sleepy," Rachel spouted. The uncles sat up, sheepish grins on their faces. James stood and put his arm around his wife.

Aria placed a hand on her stomach. "Before long, the kids will outnumber the McGuire men, and they'll be starting these dog piles."

Gabriella's gaze sought out Luke. They nodded in silent communication. "You're not exaggerating." She placed a hand on her own stomach.

Matt took a sharp inhalation as the congratulations and hugs flooded the room. He was going to have more nephews? Maybe even a niece? If he could've gone back in time, he wouldn't have allowed his family to come.

He turned to find Isabelle staring at him. Her cheeks flushed, and she looked away.

He hugged his sisters and slapped his brothers' shoulders before he approached Isabelle. "You've had enough excitement for one day," he said softly. "I'll show you your room."

"Are you sure you have enough space for me to stay here?"

He nodded and grabbed her rolling carry-on. "Come on." He wheeled it down the hallway. "You have a big day tomorrow. And don't worry about sleepwalking. You won't be able to leave without one of us stopping you."

She stared at the carpet runner. "Thank you. It's ironic that freaking out about sleepwalking can cause sleepwalking."

"You've had enough stress to last a lifetime." He stepped one foot inside her room to set down the bag and then moved back into the hallway.

"I can't thank you enough. You faced your fear of heights for me." She wrapped her arms around herself. "I think I understand that terror now."

He didn't want to talk about it. His weakness had almost stopped him from saving her life. "Thank me by staying safe."

She opened her mouth as if about to say something but then firmed her lips in one line.

"Good night, Matt." She disappeared into the room and closed the door. As he reentered the living area, everyone was calling it a night and heading for bed.

"Where are you sleeping?" Mom asked.

Matt waved at the couch near the door. "I'll be fine here." He hoped his mom didn't say anything to Isabelle about him sleeping on the couch. She'd never have agreed to stay in the suite if she'd known she'd taken his room.

"Do you want me to stay out here and help keep watch?" Mom asked.

"No, I'm fine, Mom. I promise."

She kissed his cheek. "Okay. But I'm leaving my door open to keep an ear out."

Matt agreed, checked the balcony lock and closed the curtains so he could finally relax in the living area without having to keep his gaze from the windows. He opened the door to make sure the security guard was alert outside the door before he flipped the front dead bolt. The police had a cruiser staying close by, but it didn't seem enough.

He flicked all the lights off except one dim light next to the kitchen area. The glow seeped down the hallway just enough that he could see but not enough to keep him awake or travel into any of the bedrooms. He settled his head onto one of the throw pillows and tried to make himself comfortable.

A clock in the distance ticked, as if counting down all the minutes that he couldn't fall asleep. After an hour of trying, he sat up. *It's time we chatted, Lord.* He poured out his frustrations in his prayer. Why bring Isabelle back into his life but put her in danger? Why at this time of his life, when he couldn't offer her any sort of stability? Why did He allow any of it when Matt wasn't capable of fixing anything?

Maybe it wasn't up to him.

Matt blew out a breath. Logically he knew he wasn't in control, but the knowledge didn't stop him from hating it.

A door creaked open. Matt launched to standing, his eyes wide and adjusted to the darkness.

He stepped closer to the door in case he needed to call the security guard or holler for his mom. Isabelle shuffled into the living area. She walked to the door, her hand out as if reaching for the doorknob.

"Isabelle," he whispered. "Where are you going?"

Her face turned to him, but she had a glazed, glassy-eyed expression. She blinked. "Gotta go away."

"No, you're safe," Matt whispered.

She looked right at him, and for a moment, he wondered if she had woken. "Don't throw me in the pool," she said.

He grinned, trying not to laugh while his heart felt squeezed by a strong fist. "No, I won't. I've got you. You're safe."

"I want…" Her forehead tightened, as if searching for the words.

"What do you want?" He probably shouldn't press her. He should tell her to go to bed, but he couldn't help it. His gaze dropped to her lips. She still smelled like minty toothpaste, and her dark hair swirled around her gorgeous face.

"I want…I want…" Her words came out hushed and breathy.

He took a small step toward her. It'd be wrong to kiss her awake. It'd be even worse to kiss her and not have her remember it happened. But the temptation at the moment was almost too much to bear.

"Isabelle?" His mom's voice came out of nowhere.

Matt turned to find Mom standing in her robe, one hand down at her side, most likely concealing her gun. Mom walked up to Isabelle, ignoring Matt. "Isabelle," she said softly, "go back to bed."

Isabelle's expression didn't change as she

turned slowly and walked back the way she'd come as if on automatic pilot.

Matt took a step to follow her, but Mom grabbed his arm. "Let her go."

"I just want to make sure she gets back to her room. It's an unfamiliar place."

Mom raised an eyebrow at Matt. "I'll check on her in a minute. We don't want to risk her waking up. I'm sure it was hard enough for her to fall asleep in the first place," she whispered. A few moments later, Mom followed Isabelle to make sure she had gone to bed safely.

Matt attempted to make himself comfortable on the couch once again. He punched the throw pillow until it molded to his head, but he couldn't help but feel like his mom's words had greater meaning than the situation: *Let her go.*

Their lives were both rooted in different places, and she'd made it clear she never wanted to move again. The loving thing would be not to pursue her but to let her go. Maybe they could stay in touch like Isabelle had suggested, but Matt feared if they did that, it would only make it impossible ever to find someone else. At the moment, the thought repulsed him. He didn't want anyone else. He wanted Isabelle. When marriage entered his mind, it'd always been Isabelle he thought of…and mourned. He'd have to mourn all over again.

"She still sleepwalks, huh?" Mom appeared at the foot of the couch.

"Only in times of extreme stress," he answered.

Mom huffed. "Understandable, then." She put a hand on his shoulder and prayed for peaceful sleep over the entire family and Isabelle. After she finished, she patted his head. "Just remember that worrying won't do you any good. Tomorrow has enough trouble of its own."

He sighed as she left the room. That was exactly what he was afraid of.

Isabelle hurt everywhere. Her neck, elbows and shoulders felt as if they'd gone through a towel wringer. She'd had a hard time not begging to be moved to the first floor last night. Matt's fear of heights had become her own. Every time she glanced at the windows, even with the curtains pulled, she shivered a little.

It was amazing she'd fallen asleep at all. Pure exhaustion had triumphed over worry. She stood and her stomach muscles and legs objected. Events and expectations swirled in her mind. Everything rode on the next few hours. Her presentation, catching the people responsible for terrorizing her the past week, and the need to secure an investor all rested on this day.

And yet, as she got ready, her thoughts kept flitting back to Matt. Being with his family reminded her of what kind of man he'd been raised to be…and from what she'd seen, he'd become just that. All the McGuire men were honorable and faithful. And if Matt could get over his stupid pride, he'd be much happier for it. She would love to see him implement his ideas. They would be spectacular. She was sure of it.

The suitcase was packed and secured. She'd borrowed Aria's mobile phone to check into the airline and confirm her boarding pass. Her flight was scheduled to leave two hours after the conference was done. A quiet knock at the door revealed Matt, this time dressed in a violet tie and navy suit. She inhaled. The man knew how to dress to impress.

"You almost ready?"

"Yes, thank you," she answered.

He held the door open for her. "Did you sleep okay?"

"I think so. You?"

"Couldn't get my mind off you, to be honest." His eyes met hers.

An intense desire to kiss him overwhelmed her.

"Because I was worried," he added hastily.

Oh. "Um, I'm sorry." Her voice came out in a whisper.

James poked a head around the corner. "Good. You're up. Come take a look. I'm about to go live."

On the dining-room table, her laptop hummed. Next to it, a colorful tourist map of the River Walk was spread out. Mrs. McGuire pointed to the image of her conference building. "Matt seems to think taking you by boat would be safest."

She straightened. "Boat?"

"Not that glamorous, I'm afraid. The hotel's garbage barge. I imagine whoever has been after you will expect you to go by car."

Gabriella pointed at Luke. "What if we all got wigs like Isabelle? Then Luke and his brothers could escort each of the fake Isabelles out and about as a distraction."

"Oh, I love it," Aria gushed. "Having hair like yours would be fun, Isabelle."

"No," the men said in unison.

Isabelle sucked in a breath at the power of their bass voices together. But she agreed. "I appreciate the willingness to help me, but I can't put you in danger."

"When the threat passes, I promise I'll give you an amazing tour of the area," Matt said to his family. "Until then, stay put."

Mrs. McGuire shook her head. "Your father and I are coming with you." She patted her holster. "Just in case."

"Me, too," Luke and David said in unison.

"Absolutely not. You're going to be fathers," Isabelle said.

Luke patted his own hip. "I may not brag like Mom, but I brought along some additional protection. I'm also more than capable with my firepower." Luke's gaze flitted to the twin boys as if he worked to choose his words wisely. It warmed Isabelle's heart. They would all make good parents.

Gabriella rolled her eyes. "He's pretty good. Not as good as me, but—"

"Not fair," Luke objected. "You've had more hours at the range."

She winked. "I have no doubt you'll pass me by during the next several months."

Isabelle turned to Matt. "I can't let your family—"

"I'm carrying heat, as well," Gabriella said. "I don't plan on shooting while pregnant. I don't want to risk the baby's hearing, but while you're gone, I'll be alert."

"Traveling by barge this early in the morning should be low-risk," Matt said. "Ready?"

He grabbed her carry-on for her. James tapped on the laptop. "Go now, and I'll turn on the signal. The hackers might even think you're still here. It'll be a diversion."

"What about the security cameras?" Isabelle asked. "If they still have the capability to hack, won't it be possible they'll see us leaving?"

James looked at her. "Astute observation. I've already thought of it, though." He sidestepped to a second laptop, most likely his own. His fingers flew across the keyboard. "I've remoted into the security feed myself. You're all set." He straightened. "I've been thinking, Isabelle, about what you told me of your research. I wonder if you're limiting the possibilities. Perhaps your swarm theory could help study flocks of birds, which in turn could benefit the air force, just as an example."

She shook her head. "I don't know. It really is all academic at this point, isn't it?"

He scratched his head. "I suppose so. Go break a leg."

She knew it was supposed to be encouragement for her presentation, but after the week she'd had, it didn't seem so far off to fear that very thing happening. Isabelle inhaled and followed Matt, Luke, David and their parents out the door. Lyle opened the elevator doors for them. "Knock 'em dead today, Miss Barrows."

She inwardly groaned. The last word she wanted to hear was *dead*.

The elevator opened at ground floor. Matt pointed down a hallway that was void of a carpet runner. Isabelle remembered it from the first time Matt had saved her. It was where they'd parked the barge.

Matt waved them toward another Employees Only door. "I wasn't planning on this, but Gabriella might have had a point with the disguises. Perhaps we should all wear employee overalls."

Mrs. McGuire sighed dramatically, but Isabelle followed the lead and slipped the ugly green outfit over her pantsuit. Though if anyone noticed her sequined flats underneath the hem, she'd be busted. Matt and she were the first ones at the deck of the barge, underneath a concrete overhang. Her heart pounded against her chest. It was now or never.

"Matt, listen. I want you to know how much I appreciate all you've done. Despite the circumstances, I've enjoyed the time we've had together this week."

He grinned. "Don't mention it."

"The thing is…no matter what happens with the research, I've realized something. I don't care so much about a location anymore."

He frowned. "What do you mean?"

"I mean…" She blew out a breath and looked at the calm water for inspiration to keep it together. "I like you, Matt. Instead of it decreasing over the years, it's been the opposite. You're a more mature version of the guy I fell for back then, and you said it yourself—we're more alike than we are different."

The words rushed out. Her mouth could hardly keep up with her thoughts. "With all the high-school drama far behind us, I've seen that we can be great friends, and I can't help but imagine we'd be great as even more." She sucked in a breath. His face was completely and utterly void of all expression. "I know long distance is crazy," she added, "but if you feel the same at all, I was hoping we could give us a chance."

He stood there. That was all he did. He stood, and he stared. He finally opened his mouth as if about to say something but then closed it. The metal door behind her clanged shut, and his brothers and parents appeared. When she turned back around, Matt had changed his focus to the barge tools. Her heart dropped to her stomach. Silence was perhaps the loudest answer of all.

Her throat, her ribs, her stomach all tightened. That was what she got for taking a risk. Failure. Her eyes burned as she stepped onto the barge. Well, what had she expected? He'd risked his life all week for her. She should've realized he wouldn't be crazy enough to want a relationship with her.

She blinked back the tears that threatened and focused on the cloudy skies above. If she hadn't needed to speak at the presentation, she'd have been tempted to dive in the water. At least she'd spoken her heart, like she should've done all those years ago.

She steeled herself and clenched her jaw. No more feelings. Hank was counting on her. Matt's mom stood at her back. "Okay, it's clear, Matt. Let's go."

The engine cranked and thrummed. Matt steered the barge through the small tunnel, into the hotel's lagoon of sorts. The tall buildings surrounding them did give her the illusion of safety. Except for the bridges above, they were pretty much removed from prying eyes.

Matt turned the barge around and entered the main waterway.

Crack!

The sound of a gunshot echoed as an empty trash can flew across the barge, into the control panel. David grabbed her arm and pulled her down, closest to Matt, who was hunched over. The boat swerved, and Isabelle fell into the side of Matt's leg. "Hold on," Matt yelled.

Luke was on his knees, pointing toward the bridge behind them. Mrs. McGuire scanned the area. Matt swung the boat to the right at what looked like a fork in the river.

"Isn't that the opposite direction of the convention center?" Isabelle hollered over the motor. Not that she claimed to know the area better than he did, but she'd studied the map enough to know the fastest route. Or so she thought.

"I'm worried they're waiting for us," he yelled back.

Something whizzed past her and pinged off the front of the barge. A scream ripped past her mouth before she could stop it. Instinctively she covered her ears and hunkered down. Mrs. McGuire shot off a couple of rounds at something Isabelle couldn't see.

Sirens bounced off the buildings around her. Behind them a motorboat fast approached. The driver and the passenger both looked as if they held guns. Mrs. McGuire stumbled back. "They're going to overpower us. Call the police!"

"I think they already know something is going on, Ma," David shouted back.

Luke aimed at the boat. "If you can let them pass us, I can shoot at the engine."

"They'll shoot at us before you get the chance," Mrs. McGuire yelled back.

Another boat shot around the bend about a block in front of them. They were surrounded.

FIFTEEN

Matt followed the trajectory of Isabelle's shaky finger. She pointed at the speeding boat in front of him. The driver lifted something large up and a muffled voice filled the air. A megaphone?

"It's the River Walk Patrol," Matt yelled. He didn't slow down until the police boat with three officers—one who had responded the night before—had passed them, hands at their guns. Only when they passed could they understand what was being said in the megaphone. They were telling the boat drivers to lay down their weapons.

The drivers responded by shooting back. Isabelle screamed at the sound of the guns going off. He didn't blame her. One officer ducked underneath what was probably bulletproof glass at the wheel of the boat while the other shot off a few rounds. One of the gunmen fell back into the water.

Matt slipped the barge underneath a curved bridge and pulled over. "Come on. I don't want to wait and see how the gunfight plays out. Plus we know there are more shooters around. Mom, we could use more police cover to get to the convention."

"I'm on it." Mom had a phone to her ear. They all jumped onto the sidewalk and left the barge where it was. Matt pulled Isabelle's hand as they ran up the closest set of stairs to the street.

"Isn't this too out in the open?" Isabelle yelled over the street noise.

"I have an idea," Matt said. He stepped under the closest awning. The glass door said Gliding Motor Tours. He just hoped his old buddy Chris remembered him. Matt tried to pull the door open but it was locked. He pounded on the door and looked over his shoulder.

His brothers and parents joined them. "I told the police where we were. They're on the way," his mom said. It didn't escape his notice that Luke and Mom openly held their weapons, though their fingers weren't on the triggers.

"Won't the employees think you're trying to rob them?" Isabelle asked.

Matt hoped that seeing his face would be enough to set them at ease. He jumped up, waving at the bobbing head approaching. Chris frowned, but when he saw Matt, he smiled and opened the door. "Matt! What's up, man?" Chris took in the scene behind him. "You doing some employee field trip?"

He'd forgotten they still had their overalls on. A gunshot rang out. David slammed his shoulder into Matt. "Get down!"

A ragged bullet hole in the sale banner where David had been standing remained. Chris jumped back and allowed them in the store. Though the glass door wouldn't stop bullets. Chris ran for the back door. "I need to call the police," he yelled.

"Already did," Mom called out. "They're on the way."

In the store, helmets and gliders lined the walls. Gliding Motors was an off-brand model similar to a Segway. Tourists rented them as a fun way to see all the sights without having to worry about parking, traffic or sore feet.

They ran into a back room. Chris shoved a door behind them and locked it. "Matt, I'd do anything for you, but there's someone with a gun out there."

He didn't need him to state the obvious. "Let me rent some of these and go out the back way. You should lock up and go next door until the danger passes. You have my word I'll pay for any damages."

Chris pulled his eyebrows together. "Only for you, man."

Matt grabbed his outstretched hand and slapped his shoulder at the same time. "Do me a favor and take off the speed limiter."

Chris raised an eyebrow but typed in a code into the displays of the gliders in the back. "I've got only four."

"We'll make do."

"They're not meant for two people, you know."

Matt nodded at Isabelle. "You'll have to lean back hard when I tell you to stop to compensate."

The sound of bullets and breaking glass reached their ears. "They're coming. Chris, go now. At this rate, the gunmen will beat the police by several minutes."

Isabelle watched Matt's dad hop on a glider and his mom put her legs between his with one arm around his waist. Isabelle's eyes widened, and she pointed at Matt. "I'm riding with you?"

He turned on the motor. "No time for second-guessing, Izzy." His stance on the glider shifted slightly as she stepped up to join him. Her arms wrapped around his waist.

There was no time to enjoy the sensation of having her this close to him. He leaned forward and sped down the ramp, out of the store. "Are they following me?" he hollered.

"Your family? Yeah."

Never before had he been so thankful to know the area like the back of his hand. He traveled everywhere on foot. He knew every shortcut and alley to be found. The first left he took went between two buildings and would take them through La Vallita Historic Arts Village.

The scents of chocolate croissants and coffee wafted past as he pressed the glider to its maximum speed. This was exactly one of the sights he felt sure Isabelle would've loved if she had the freedom to walk around safely. The hum behind him meant his brothers and dad were keeping up.

Sirens wailed in the distance, but they couldn't afford to wait for the police. Not after they'd been shot at several times. Two motorcycles jumped the curb and drove straight for them. One driver lifted a gun.

Crack!

The driver of the first bike fell backward as the motorcycle fell over, sliding right for him. The second motorcycle spun around, changing course. Matt veered to the right, barely squeezing between two of the galleries.

"Your mom shot the guy's front tire!"

Matt's entire insides shook. He was glad he never had seen his mom in action before, because the thought of her dealing with criminals terrified him. He chanced a glance over his shoulder. His brothers, dad and mom had made the sharp turn right behind him. His mom held her gun up, one arm around his dad.

Behind the galleries were other art shops, thankfully not open yet. Going at top speed—over twenty miles an hour, if he had to guess—they'd make it back to the sidewalk in less than a minute.

"Matt," Isabelle yelled.

At the end of the buildings, a motorcycle revved up to the entrance. The driver put one foot down and shot. Matt's torso pulled back sharply. Isabelle was pulling him back, taking them down. And there was no way to warn his brothers.

A searing pain shot across the back of Isabelle's arm. She'd arched her back with the sudden shock. The abrupt move flung both her and Matt completely off the glider. Her backside bounced against the cement as her left hand tried to stabilize. The brunt of impact came from Matt's head, which hit her shoulder before he rolled away.

The other gliders were going full speed behind them. She lifted her head to see Luke turn the handles at ninety degrees. The glider spun in a circle before throwing him against the side of the building. David and Mr. McGuire hollered but screeched to a stop before they ran over either of them.

"Are you okay?" Matt panted.

"Stay down!" Mrs. McGuire jumped in front of Matt's dad and fired. The motorcycle driver revved around, and in the cycle's place, a flashing ATV covered the alley exit. *Protecting the Alamo City* was written underneath the SAPD logo.

Matt reached for her. "You've been shot."

She glanced down at the rip in the overalls. The wound hurt, but it wasn't overwhelming like she'd imagined the pain of a bullet. "I think maybe I'm just scratched?"

David scoffed, "You sound like a McGuire." He reached out a hand to a fallen Luke, who gladly accepted. Aside from messed-up hair, Luke seemed relatively unharmed.

Mrs. McGuire rushed to check each of them. "If a bullet didn't graze you, something ricocheted."

While her arm started to throb, Isabelle was thankful she had something covering her sleeves to take some of the force, since she had on a sleeveless blouse and trousers underneath. Her right flat had flown off with the fall.

"Weapons down," someone yelled from the

other end of the alley. Two officers on bicycles approached. Mrs. McGuire made a great showing of putting down her gun.

"She's not a threat," Matt hollered.

The ATV policeman explained that the Park Patrol had been shot at on the boats. "As such, we've been authorized to grant you a police escort to the conference for your presentation."

Isabelle sighed. It was about time something went right.

"And afterward, to the airport," the officer added.

Matt exhaled. No doubt he couldn't wait until she was long gone. She strained to smile at the McGuire family. "Go with her," Mr. McGuire told Matt. "We'll take the gliders back with the other officers."

"Send the glider bill to me, Dad," Matt said.

"You don't have to come, Matthew," Isabelle said.

He put a hand on her back. "Let's see this thing through. Officer, do you have a first-aid kit?"

A car pulled up behind the ATV. Their ride had arrived.

Isabelle tried not to be affected by his touch in the squad car. She'd taken off the overalls as he cleaned up the bleeding with a wipe and attached a butterfly bandage to her wound. Too bad she didn't have anything else to cover up the wound before her presentation. In the scope of things, it just didn't matter. "I don't have any identification, and I haven't had time to stop by the station yet. Will that be a problem for the airlines?"

"I have a written police report with me you can present the TSA. It shouldn't be a problem." The officer pulled up to the front doors of the conference center.

Isabelle could see the looks of concern from her colleagues within as the officer opened the car for her. In their shoes, she probably wouldn't know what to think if the keynote speaker for the morning showed up in the backseat of a cop car. "I don't suppose you could escort me inside and tell everyone the limo was in the shop."

The officer chuckled as Matt joined her. "Just tell them oceanology is dangerous."

She sighed. "Truth."

"I'll remain here until after your presentation, Miss Barrows," the officer said.

"Oh, wait. My suitcase… Is it long gone?"

"Ideally it's still on the barge. I'll make sure it's retrieved and brought here," Matt said.

"Thank you." She stepped inside only to find security guards flanking the main hall. She didn't recall any guards the other times she attended.

Sandra Parveen rushed to meet her. "You're still going to present?"

Isabelle nodded. "It won't be as fancy as I'd hoped, but it'll get the job done."

"A word, Miss Barrows," a voice boomed. Allen strode to meet her.

"I'll meet you backstage to go over your introduction." Parveen tapped her wrist and pointed to a hallway. "Be there in ten minutes."

"Understood." Isabelle's heart pounded. So much was happening at once, she feared her entire speech and knowledge had left her completely. What if she stood on the podium in front of two hundred of the greatest scientists in her field and had nothing of value to say?

"I want to know why the police thought I had something to do with an attack on you," Allen said.

Struther crossed the crowded room. "I'm curious about that, as well. I got a second visit from the police last night. As far as I knew, the police absolved me of all suspicion after the Tower incident. So why—"

"Oh, I wonder." Matt's tone reeked of sarcasm. "You two are obviously in cahoots about something. And Allen has a better idea of what her research entails than anyone else here."

Isabelle's cheeks heated. Allen was highly respected in the industry, and if Matt offended him, then she could kiss her last shot at an investor goodbye.

Allen and Struther exchanged a glance. Struther clapped his hands together. "Well, we had to tell the police, anyway. I suppose it won't hurt to tell you in confidence. I'm about to be promoted to CEO, and as such, I'm looking to put Endangered Robotics underneath our umbrella."

"But you're nonprofit," Isabelle objected to Allen.

He shrugged. "We've just come to an agreement. It would be a beneficial partnership. We'll remain separate entities but underneath one roof. Robotic Aquatic could do the research and development on the profit side, then pass on the licensed stuff to the nonprofit side of the company. I've been trying to convince Struther to invest in your institute, Isabelle, under the nonprofit arm. That way it doesn't carry as much risk, with the provision that we merge with Hayden Research so you can work for us. We can see a lot of potential use on both sides for your research."

Isabelle's mouth dropped open. She blinked rapidly in an attempt to process. All this time those two had been fighting because they'd been trying to merge their nonprofit and profit companies? She could handle the stipulation, but the idea that her uncle would need to give up Hayden Research Station… She closed her eyes. At the moment it didn't matter, because the truth was, he might be losing it anyway.

"We're still ironing out some of the legalities," Struther said. "But prepare for a nice offer this afternoon if your presentation is anything close to what Allen tells me. And in return, maybe keep the police from knocking on my door?"

They walked away. She almost told them that someone had stolen the research, but until the mysterious thief acquired the encryption key, she still had hope.

Matt put a hand on her arm. She flinched as if burned. His touch was just a reminder that he didn't want her. She didn't want a moment alone to hear him even utter the words.

"I need to go. Excuse me." She stepped toward the hallway Parveen had indicated.

"But, Izzy—"

"Thank you, Matthew."

"Goodbye, Isabelle. It was good to see you again."

She blinked back the tears and opened the door that led into the darkened hallway next to the backstage area. Her fingers pressed against her tear ducts as she inhaled. It would be fine. Life would go back to normal.

And even with her research gone, she could re-create it. If someone else had it, it wasn't as valuable, but maybe she would discover something else or progress faster. The danger would ideally be gone the moment she touched down at the Portland airport. It would all work out. She just needed to cling to her original goals before her heart had gotten involved.

She opened the door to the backstage area. As soon as Parveen went over the schedule and introduction, Isabelle would enjoy fifteen minutes of peace and quiet to get her head on straight. The presentation still needed to blow Struther and Allen out of the water. And sure, if Hayden Research got bought out, she might not get to keep some of the favorite aspects of her job—like leading the educational field trips to the tide pools or working alongside her uncle. But now wasn't the time to think on any of it, or the empty feeling at the thought of losing Matt McGuire...again.

She stepped inside a little room on the side of the stage. It seemed odd there were no lights on. "Ms. Parveen?" she called out. Come to think of it, it seemed odd the way Parveen asked if she was still going to present today. Isabelle had told no one other than the police and the McGuires that her research had been stolen.

She hadn't even called to update Hank yet. So why would Parveen ask?

An ominous click sounded behind her as the door shut.

The light flickered and blinded her momentarily. Sandra Parveen had duct tape over her mouth, and her hands were zip-tied behind the back of a chair. The man at the door pointed a gun directly at Isabelle's chest. "Hello, Miss Barrows." He smirked. "Or perhaps I should say, goodbye."

SIXTEEN

Matt paced the lobby of the conference center. He'd called David about Isabelle's bag and to get an update on the honey pot. So far James hadn't seen so much as a nibble from any hackers. David said he'd already retrieved her carry-on bag and was on his way to deliver it to the officer who would drive her to the airport.

He'd been looking forward to attending Isabelle's famed presentation, but after their interaction this morning, he worried he would be an unwelcome distraction. He couldn't bear to ruin her big day. His heart beat faster as he recalled her words on the barge.

Isabelle was willing to give them a chance, as more than friends. And he had just stood there like an idiot until he was sure she regretted ever saying a word. But what could he have said? If he admitted he had feelings for her, then she might give up her dream for him. He'd never forgive himself if she did that.

And then, on top of it all, if he ended up having to move around, feelings of resentment would build until she couldn't stand him. He needed at least to explain why he hadn't said anything, but how could he do that without admitting he had fallen hard for her?

David walked in empty-handed. "The cop put her bag in the car. What a day, right?" He shoved his hands into his pockets and looked out the expansive windows. "You know, I came here hoping you were ready to realize your true potential."

Matt pulled his chin in. "What are you talking about?"

"You'd take one look at us and what we've become, wake up and beg to be schooled in the empire we're building. Instead, you're here and so happy that we couldn't possibly expect you to consider—"

"Isabelle told you." Matt shook his head. "Unbelievable."

David smirked. "Of course she did. Can't get anything past your big brother."

Matt stepped closer so his brother was forced to look him in the eye. "What exactly did she say?"

David smiled. "She said that someday you hoped to run my new California conference center."

He folded his arms across his chest. "She had no right."

"If it were anyone else, I'd agree with you, but Izzy was practically family before she moved away. She knows you. And I've been told my smoldering eyes can get anyone to talk."

"Isabelle," Matt said.

David raised an eyebrow. "What?"

"She wants to be called Isabelle. Only I get to call her Izzy." The last sentence came out of his mouth in the heat of the moment. If only he could redact it. "And you probably looked like a lost puppy. My eyes could out-smolder you any day."

A slow smile crossed David's face. "Okay. Straight up? I said I had hoped you didn't like it here so much. I practically baited her into telling me."

That made more sense. "Well, you can forget it. It's not how I want this to go down. Besides, Isabelle got it wrong. I was more interested in the Oregon conference center."

David laughed. "I wondered. Isn't Sand Dollar Shores only twenty minutes from where she lives?"

"That's not why." Matt's chest heated. Was it really that close? That was less time than most people commuted.

David turned back to face the window. "I've got my pride, too, Matt. I think it's in the McGuire DNA. Although, personally I think it's more about dignity and less about self-righteousness, but I might be fooling myself. I wonder sometimes…maybe God hates the proud because He knows it keeps us not only from seeking Him but also from letting others know what we want." David shrugged. "But what do I know?" He slapped Matt on the back. "I've been my own worst enemy before, little brother. Don't make the same mistake I did. Let her know."

Matt shook his head. "What are you talking about now?" It drove him nuts when any of his brothers added the word *little*.

David laughed. "I'm going to see if I can find some coffee." He shook his head and walked away without any further explanation.

Matt's phone vibrated. He flipped it open and James started talking before he even offered a greeting. "They've already found the honey pot. They're using a satellite connection, which is harder for me to trace accurately, but I think the signal is coming from inside the conference center. Matt, they're attacking the system with everything they've got. I need to pull it offline before they find the real encryption.

Keep Isabelle close. She's probably in danger just being there."

Matt hung up the phone and started running toward the hallway he'd last seen Isabelle walk toward. David must've seen his movement, because he sprinted to his side. "She went through that door."

Two giant security guards appeared out of nowhere and stepped in front of the door. "No access, sir."

David and Matt exchanged glances. No one was keeping him from getting to Isabelle. No one.

Isabelle pulled her shoulders back and forced herself to stare into Mr. Frazer's eyes. "I take it you were never interested in booking the hotel." She stared at him, recalling the past week and all the places she'd seen him.

He'd been asleep in the lobby—obviously faking, now that she thought about it—after the Tower incident. Had that meant he was actually after her laptop then? And he'd been in the hotel before and after the elevator incident. He'd been joking with the guards after she'd almost been gunned down. Perhaps to sneak a peek at the security system? And he'd stood behind her when she was talking to Struther and Allen about the flash drive. In fact, he'd stood next to the front desk when Matt had instructed the staff to move her to the suite. The man had always been in the background, watching…and most likely directing his associates.

Frazer nodded. "Astute observation." His voice was filled with sarcasm. He pointed at a chair opposite Parveen.

If he tied her hands behind the chair, she'd be sunk. Her dad had run her through similar situations. Except it was harder to recall what to do when it came down to it. She sat down and, without waiting for instructions, put her elbows together, leaned forward and offered her wrists to Frazer. She tucked her chin down and closed her eyes so as to appear submissive. "Please don't duct-tape my mouth," she begged. "I promise I'll cooperate."

"Look at that, Ms. Parveen. See how easy it could've been for you if you'd had a little manners?" Frazer's voice sounded sinister, but he didn't rip Isabelle's arms backward. He yanked the cold plastic tight against her wrists and shoved her shoulders back into the chair. "For now the duct tape stays off, but not because you asked. I might need you, but if I hear one squawk out of you, you'll get a lot more than duct tape. Understood?"

Isabelle knew enough not to answer. Frazer straightened and moved to a small desk in the far corner, where a dimly lit laptop was running through lines of code. "In just a moment I'll have what I need and this will all be over."

Parveen let out a squeak behind the duct tape. Isabelle assumed Parveen understood that *over* meant *dead*.

"So, at least give me some peace of mind," Isabelle said softly. "Why you? You're not even in the industry. Are you?"

Frazer smirked. He set his gun down for a second as he typed a few lines into the laptop. The faint light from the screen glinted off the sparkling half of her necklace. So he had the flash drive. "I'm in a different type of industry. Ms. Parveen actually hired my organization's services to acquire your research and kill you."

Isabelle flinched. Parveen had been behind it all along? She had been standing right behind her in the Tower, talking with Matt, when Struther set up a meeting with her. She knew the conference schedule and where Isabelle was staying. But why would she do it? Parveen wouldn't meet her gaze.

"Oh, yes," Frazer continued. "Apparently the conference business gives her access to all sorts of new research she can sell to the highest bidder. Whatever you stumbled on was worth a very nice asking price." Frazer tapped on the computer.

The collar of his shirt gaped a bit, revealing part of a tattoo on his chest. She recognized it. The man in the cab had it. Did they all have it? How many people was she up against?

"So nice a price that I felt the need to take over the auction myself." Frazer shook a finger at Isabelle. "But I must admit, you gave me a run for my money. I usually get to stay on the sidelines and dispatch my associates. But you're a smart one. A challenge worthy of some personal attention."

"You're trying to get the security encryption," Isabelle said.

Frazer pursed his lips. "And I might consider not killing Ms. Parveen if you help me access it."

Parveen made a loud squeal underneath the duct tape. Frazer picked up his gun and shot her in a seamless motion. A ping came from the gun's silencer. Isabelle flinched against the back of her chair and couldn't help a small squeak coming out of her own mouth. Parveen's shoulder began bleeding as she hunched over, tears falling.

Frazer scowled. "I told her to be quiet. Though if you don't care about her life, maybe I can grab another conference attendee. I have plenty of bullets."

Logically she understood Parveen had been

the one to hire a hit on her life in the first place. If Frazer could be believed. But she couldn't ignore the woman in extreme pain sitting across from her. An attempt to bluff and act as if she didn't care if Frazer killed Parveen could give her an opportunity to escape, but Frazer seemed the type to call her bluff in a heartbeat. She didn't want Parveen's death on her conscience. She needed to buy them time.

Soon she would be expected on the stage to give the presentation. If she were late to the stage, then someone would come looking for her. She just needed to stall. *Please let Matt have the sense to alert the police before coming after me.*

"I can enable the security encryption key," she said slowly. "But it's too complicated to explain."

He narrowed his eyes. "Try me."

Isabelle struggled to recall exactly what she'd said when she'd made the gunman in the Tower falter. "I used a quantum permanent compromise attack. I used the equation if x is—"

"Yes, I know all that. You don't need to bore me with meaningless equations."

Isabelle was the one to falter. He knew? She took in a small breath. He was the one the gunman had called in the Tower.

"You don't skip the hierarchy and take over

an underground criminal organization without some smarts, Miss Barrows. Now, want to try again? Or shall I use up another bullet?"

She swallowed. There was no bluffing Frazer, then. She knew it was smarter to stay in one location and wait for help, but time was ticking. "Do you have my phone or my tablet with you?"

He narrowed his eyes. "So you can play some Tetris?"

Studies showed a daily dose of Tetris increased brain efficiency, but she pursed her lips to keep a defensive comeback from flying out. "There's a back door on each device that when combined... Well, you apparently know." The truth was, she didn't know if it was even possible to set up such a system, but she just needed him to consider it to buy some time. Frazer raised an eyebrow.

The door burst open. Two guards stood on either side of Matt, who had a growing black eye. A small cry escaped from her lips.

"We have a problem," the guard on the left said. "One of them got away. Ran straight outside to the police."

"Is it our guy?" Frazer asked.

Isabelle's mouth dropped. The police were under his thumb, also?

"I think so," the guard answered. "He was the one waiting outside for her."

Frazer gave her a look. "See, we had a backup plan." He tapped his temple.

"So you can kill me sooner rather than later?" The question flew out of her mouth before she could stop it.

"I would think you would care more about who else I took out until I have what I wanted." He pointed to one guard. "Go see if the officer needs your assistance in damage control."

Her blood ran cold. What did "damage control" mean? Had innocent bystanders seen anything? Matt's face paled, as well.

"We're about out of time anyway." Frazer pointed the gun and silenced Sandra Parveen forever.

Isabelle cried out and began to shake.

"Would you like to reconsider the duct tape, Miss Barrows?"

She clamped her mouth shut and took sharp inhalations in an attempt to stop the shaking.

"We're going to take a little field trip since your friend here caused some unwanted attention. If you do anything to add to that attention, Mr. McGuire here will be the next to suffer. I hope I've made myself clear."

SEVENTEEN

The remaining security guard wrenched Matt's arm backward and placed a zip tie around his wrists. Across the room, Mr. Frazer stuffed a laptop in a bag. Isabelle hunched over her arms, presumably crying, but her mouth grabbed the end of the zip tie and tugged.

Matt almost told her it would do no good, but she seemed to have another purpose. She stopped when the square lock on the tie lined up between her wrists. Her eyes lifted to the lifeless form of Parveen and then darted to him.

His only hope would be that the cop wouldn't try anything at the front of the conference center, where people were walking by at all times and security cameras were positioned. Though if Frazer had two security guards and a cop under his thumb, maybe that wasn't enough to guarantee David's safety.

Frazer had succeeded in keeping Matt's guard down at the hotel because he'd appealed to his pride. His neck tingled and his stomach churned with the reality of how well it'd worked. David was right. Dignity was one thing, but Matt had let pride supersede wisdom. He hadn't come clean with Isabelle so they could figure out the possibility of a relationship together. He hadn't been a straight shooter with David and the rest of the family from the beginning about his hopes and dreams for the conference center at Sand Dollar Shores.

"Let's go get your phone and tablet, Miss Barrows," Frazer said. "Don't worry. It's close by, and if I find it doesn't solve my problem, you'll be very sorry." He jutted his head to the security guard. "Clean this up." He gestured with his gun for Matt and Isabelle to walk ahead of him into the darkened hallway.

The crackle of a speaker sounded in the room behind them. "Sir," the guard called out. "His brothers are arriving. They're entering the building."

Matt's eyes widened in the darkness. That meant his entire family would be in danger, but it also ideally meant David had a chance of survival. Luke would at least have a weapon.

"Deploy the rest of the team. Keep it discreet."

He wanted it discreet? Then Matt needed to make sure they did the opposite. What was it that Isabelle always cited? OODA? Observe, Orient, Decide, Act. His eyes strained to see anything they could act with.

Aside from folding chairs lined up against the auditorium hallway, there was nothing. Music and loud conversations filtered through the wall, which meant that hundreds of attendees were waiting for the keynote presentation to start. Even if they screamed their heads off, it was unlikely anyone would hear them over all the noise. "Now would be a great time for OODA," he whispered.

She turned her wide eyes to him. She nodded. "Do you hear that?" she said aloud.

"What?" Frazer snapped.

She swung her bound wrists above her head and pulled them down fast and hard. Her right elbow shoved back into Frazer at the same time a slight pop sounded and the zip tie flew off her wrists. Matt couldn't mimic the motion, but maybe he could try something similar. Either way, he wasn't about to let Frazer shoot her.

He stomped on Frazer's foot and shoved his entire body into his side. Frazer hit the wall. A ping echoed in the hall as Isabelle yanked at something unseen in the wall. Fire-alarm sirens filled the building.

Matt leaned his torso forward, swung his arms as far up as he could strain, then swung them down. His fists hit his own backside painfully hard, but his elbows spread apart with the momentum. The zip tie strained against his wrists but didn't budge. Frazer shoved him to the side and straightened, taking aim at Isabelle. Matt kicked him in the stomach.

The gun dropped. Matt kicked it down the hall and tried to swing his arms up again. As he swung downward, the zip tie snapped, stinging his wrists.

Isabelle grabbed a folding chair and spun around, slamming the chair into Frazer. He buckled. Matt pulled his fist back and let it fly into his torso. Frazer fell back, and Matt and Isabelle both took off running. A creak behind them made Matt look over his shoulder into the darkness. Had the security guard in the room come out?

A flash of light. "Get down!"

He shoved her head down as the ping of a gun sounded uncomfortably close to his ear. Matt slammed into the door leading to the lobby area as another ping went off and Frazer yelled something. The light overwhelmed his senses, but he pressed forward, shoving Isabelle in front of him, into the throng of people flooding the entrance.

"No shoving," an irritated man yelled at Matt.

"Matt," a voice yelled over the crowd. It sounded like Luke…or David.

"Matt," another voice screamed. That one definitely belonged to his mother.

Two men in suits grabbed Isabelle and Matt. Matt spun around, his knee in motion to smash into the guy's stomach, when he heard "NSA."

Matt tried to slow down the momentum, but the man was able to sidestep him. "Show me a badge!"

"They're legit," Isabelle hollered over the fire alarm. She waved a badge above her head.

A dozen more men in suits scattered in various locations around the lobby. Several more stood at the entrance, checking identifications before allowing attendees to leave.

"You set off the fire alarm?" the agent asked.

She nodded meekly.

"Good." The agent spoke into a small device. "No fire threat." A moment later the sirens stopped. The music in the background also halted, and a voice came over the speakers explaining that this was just a fire drill. The conference would resume in a moment. Several attendees grumbled and returned back to the auditorium.

"The cop out there is dirty," Matt hollered.

"Sir, we've got him. Agent McGuire has already briefed us on the threat situation."

That statement almost took his breath away. Agent McGuire? He thought James had retired years ago. Had he joined the agency again after his own run-in with danger?

Frazer stumbled into the room, wearing handcuffs, with agents flanking each of his sides. Isabelle sidestepped the agent and ran toward him. Matt ran after her, fearing she would do something she regretted.

Isabelle pulled her necklace out of the laptop bag that another agent held. "I'll take this."

Matt blew out a breath. "I thought you were going to attack him."

The thought resonated with her. Frazer had made the last week a nightmare she would do anything to forget. Although if Matt had thought she would attack the man, she was surprised he had followed her. She smiled, remembering what he'd said in the Tower staircase. "I bring the crazy, you bring the muscle?"

He shrugged. "Maybe something like that."

The agent pointed to the necklace. "Agent McGuire alerted us to the potential of your research. After your presentation, if we believe it pertains to national security, we will set up a joint meeting with the Department of Defense."

Isabelle placed a hand on her chest. "I still get to make my presentation?"

The agent nodded. "Yes, ma'am. The sooner, the better."

She gripped the flash drive in both hands, and her eyes glistened. There was still potential to save the institute and her uncle's financial security. "Are you sure I'll be out of danger?"

The agent pursed his lips. "We believe we've neutralized both threats."

"Both?"

"We tracked down two bidders. Rumors of your research threatened a billion-dollar contract between the US Navy and a weapons manufacturer on the East Coast. It would've made the drone technology they've invested millions on in R & D irrelevant. The second bidder was an organization that's been very vocal about tracking and eliminating navy submarines in foreign waters."

Her stomach plummeted.

"So we have a vested interest now in your presentation," the agent finished.

Her heart pounded so hard it rang in her ears. Or it could have been that she couldn't get the fire-alarm siren sound out of her mind. Either way, there was so much to process and no time to do so if she was going to give her presentation. There was still hope she could come through for Uncle Hank, and her research could be used for good. She pointed to the auditorium. "I'm not going through the back entrance again."

The agent nodded. "Understood."

"Okay, then I'm ready."

"Isabelle, wait." Matt reached across the space between them and touched her wrist. His thumb brushed over the red lines created from the friction of the zip tie when she broke it. "About earlier. I'm sorry I didn't speak right away. I—"

Here it came. The "I just want to be friends" speech she knew was coming after his silence on the barge earlier today. After watching someone die in front of her eyes and narrowly escaping their own deaths, she just couldn't take another emotional blow.

"It's okay, Matt." She spotted his family members fighting their way through the crowds to get to them. She especially didn't want to hear this speech in front of them. It'd be too humiliating. "We're good. No words necessary."

Mrs. McGuire pulled her into a hug and then grabbed Matt with her other arm. She released both of them at the same time. "Don't you dare scare me like that again. Either one of you."

"It's not like we planned it, Ma," Matt objected.

James, Luke and David joined their circle. "Don't even bother trying," Luke said. "She thinks we all planned to fall into danger."

"And the least we could do was give her twenty-four-hour notice," David sassed.

"What can we say, Mom?" James asked. "We just wanted to follow in your footsteps and bring about justice to the world."

Mrs. McGuire's face melted into a smile. She patted James's cheek. "Nice try. No dessert for any of you since you took a few years off my life."

As the rest of the boys objected and argued they were grown men, James lifted a laptop bag off his shoulder. "I believe this is yours, Isabelle."

"How'd you get the NSA here?"

He threw a thumb over his shoulder. "They have a main office here in San Antonio. I'm grateful they still listen to me as a consultant."

"I can't thank you enough."

James pointed at the flash drive in her hand. "Actually, you can. Keep me in the loop. I think there are some possible space applications in what you've got started there."

"Miss Barrows, they're ready for you." Another agent stood by. She nodded and stepped away from Matt with a smile. His eyes looked soft and thoughtful, but she couldn't stay any longer. She headed for the stage, where she would force herself to think of nothing but equations and numbers. Otherwise, she'd fall apart. Leaving Matt felt like moving away... all over again.

EIGHTEEN

It'd been a long two weeks. Matt had to endure his family pouncing on him the moment Isabelle left. *"What's wrong with you? Go after her."* It was an intervention of sorts. Though they quieted the moment he agreed they were right.

Matt had gone through the motions at work and gave his family a presentation of what he'd like to accomplish in Sand Dollar Shores. After some teasing, David and Aria offered him the position on the spot. The victory seemed hollow without being able to tell Isabelle.

He had called Isabelle's research institute. They informed him Isabelle was taking a little time off. Understandable after everything that had happened. But she'd be returning to work as a hero. The DoD had fast-tracked her proposal, so her research was now fully funded without needing any help from Struther or Allen.

Uncle Hank had mercy on him the fifth time

he'd called, though, and gave him Isabelle's phone number.

Matt had tried calling, but she hadn't picked up. He'd tried texting, but she always sent back short replies. When he gave her congratulations for the funding, she texted back, Thx. He messaged her that she was right about being up front with his brother about what he wanted. She merely replied, I'm glad.

So as Matt stood in the parking lot of Hayden Research Station, he had no idea how his arrival would be received. His insides shook a little. He normally only did things when he felt sure he knew the outcome. Laying down his pride was harder than he thought it'd be.

The wind carried the sound of the ocean waves crashing against the shore. The soothing smell of the salt air emboldened him. Hank had passed along her schedule for the day, so Matt knew she would be about to lead a classroom among the tide pools. He'd even asked the teacher if she could wait for a few minutes, and she'd agreed. It was now or never.

He pulled the front door open and walked past the front aquarium into the laboratory. Isabelle stood next to the wall of windows, the ocean view at her back. The sun highlighted her dark hair with its many highlights. She wore a lab coat over a periwinkle blouse and navy-blue skirt. His chest constricted. Even after two weeks apart, he knew without a doubt he loved her with all his heart.

Her blue eyes lifted, and her mouth gaped. "Matt? What are you doing here?"

He gulped and attempted to flash a charming smile. "I heard you had a crush on someone."

Her face fell. "Matt—"

Okay, probably not the best way to start. He took a step forward. "I told this Matt guy he needed to know a few things about you."

Her eyebrows lifted and her right hand flew to her chest. "If you think this is funny—" She shook her head. "I don't have time for this. I have a school group."

This was all going so wrong. In his head it was romantic, but this wasn't how it was supposed to play out. "Isabelle, let me fin—"

"I have to go." She darted out the back door. Through the glass walls, he could see the children look up and form a line. His plan was falling apart. He just hoped she'd hear him out. He ran back out the front door and around the building.

Isabelle's throat constricted. How was she supposed to teach the group about tide pools when her eyes were blurry with tears? She blinked them back. Why was Matt even here?

To make sure their friendship was okay? Because if he thought he could joke about her declaration so soon...

She swallowed and did a double take. Why had the children formed a line? Their teacher was at the far end, closest to some of the big monolith rocks, and she was smiling. Maybe the teacher thought this was what Isabelle wanted from the class?

Apparently the teacher didn't get the email she'd sent about what to expect on the field trip. Isabelle smiled at the students and took a step forward. The first child pulled a rose from behind his back and handed it to her.

She faltered. "Oh. Wow. Uh...thank you." She took another step forward, and the second child pulled a rose from behind her back. Isabelle's heart raced. Down the line, all the children had their hands behind their backs and beamed with expectant grins and giggles. What was going on?

As she walked slowly, closer and closer to the ocean, each child handed her a rose. The smell of salt water mixed with the heady scent of roses was delicious. The bouquet grew to almost two dozen flowers. Isabelle reached the teacher, who smiled and pointed over Isabelle's shoulder.

Matt stepped around the monolith rock, his eyes downcast.

"Matt?" She turned back to the children. The teacher had ushered them back into a group.

"I'm sorry I upset you, Isabelle." His voice sounded strained. "It's going to sound silly now, but I had it all planned out. Please let me finish, and then if you want me to stop and leave, I will."

She tilted her head but remained silent.

"I wanted to tell you that I warned this Matt guy about you. I told him how intense you were...the kind of intensity that inspires you to be the best you can be. She has this way of questioning everything...a love of discovery and learning that's contagious."

She sucked in a breath. He was repeating everything he'd said to Randy all those years ago, except listing all the positive aspects.

"And she's stubborn...the kind of determination and loyalty and perseverance that is so rare to find in a person. And so intelligent and brilliant, yet open-minded and humble enough never to look down on anyone else.

"The thing is," Matt went on, "it didn't matter what I said to him. The moment he opened his heart, he was a goner. He'd never be able to get her out of his mind." He took a step forward. "Do you still want me to stop?" he whispered.

"I might let you go on," she murmured. "Only if you promise to stop talking about yourself in the third person."

He beamed. "I don't have a crush on you," Matt said. "It goes way beyond that, Isabelle. I love you." His words came out fast, in a rush. He lifted his eyes, questioning.

She blinked. He really didn't know? "I love you, Matthew."

His hands caressed her cheek as he leaned forward and kissed her.

She tilted her chin to stare into his eyes. "But if you felt that way about me, then why—"

"When you told me you wanted to give us a shot, I was too scared I'd mess things up. I wasn't sure how to answer until I figured some things out."

There was giggling in the background and what sounded like splashing. Matt stepped back. "This didn't really go as planned," he said apologetically.

Isabelle followed his gaze as four kayaks glided into view. The boats fought the waves to get in a line. Isabelle squinted. "Are those your brothers?"

"And my dad." Matt gave a sheepish grin.

The men held up signs with one hand as their boats were carried by the waves toward them.

Isabelle tried to read the bobbing signs. "'You Will Marry Me'?"

"Ah, no." He slapped his forehead. "David and Luke got out of order."

His words barely registered. She turned back to Matt. He lowered himself down on one knee.

"Isabelle Barrows, I know this is fast, but I also know no matter how long I need to wait, you are the only woman for me."

Stunned, she studied his face. The vulnerability and uncertainty were written in his eyes. He was risking his pride to tell her what he wanted. Her heart swelled.

"Will you make me the happiest man on earth and be my wife…eventually? Whenever you're ready?"

She laughed. "Oh, I'm ready." She fought the swelling of her throat and nodded. "Yes. Yes, I will marry you."

He jumped up and grabbed her by the waist. The roses slipped from her hands, swirling around her as he spun her in the air and pulled her into his arms. His lips met hers. She pressed into him, knowing there was nothing pretend about this kiss. The schoolchildren released a mixed chorus of disgusted groans and happy cheers.

Matt straightened and set her down as Mrs. McGuire, Rachel, Gabriella and Aria ran out from behind other distant rocks. The kayaks slid onto shore as the men also rushed to join them.

James swooped one of the twins in his arms as Rachel picked up the other. "She going to be our new aunt, huh?" The twins both nodded at the same time.

Isabelle laughed. "Yes. I would love to be your new aunt."

Aria hugged her. "Be careful what you say. There are future nieces and nephews to come."

Isabelle laughed and embraced everyone but had no words. She was too happy.

Aria threw a thumb over her shoulder at the group of kids. "David and I have been tide-pool guides a few times. Do you mind if we take this one?"

Isabelle nodded, and Aria led the rest of the McGuire family away toward the class.

Isabelle couldn't stop smiling, except then the thought of being engaged yet living so far apart began to sink in. She sighed. "Matt, I can't leave here for a few years. I signed a contract. I was willing to do long distance, and I still am." She frowned. "I'll figure something out. We'll make it work. We can do this."

Matt tilted his head. "I think I forgot to clarify something. I don't want to run David's new conference center."

"You don't?" Traveling back and forth to San Antonio would be harder than Northern California, but it didn't matter. Maybe she could rent an office in San Antonio and do some of her work there if—

"I want to run the one twenty minutes from here."

Her eyes searched his. "No prank?"

He pulled her in tighter. "This is definitely no prank." He leaned down and his lips met hers. And in his arms she knew. She was home.

* * * * *

If you enjoyed TEXAS TAKEDOWN
by Heather Woodhaven,
look for these other books by the author:

CALCULATED RISK
SURVIVING THE STORM
CODE OF SILENCE
COUNTDOWN

Available now from Love Inspired Suspense!
Find more great reads at
www.LoveInspired.com

Dear Reader,

Two years ago, my husband had a work trip scheduled for San Antonio in June. As our twentieth anniversary was fast approaching, my husband's parents agreed to come watch the children so I could take the opportunity to travel with him. It was such a blessing. I knew Matt McGuire, the final brother, had been working hard as a hotel manager somewhere, waiting for me to tell his story.

While my husband was at his conference, I explored. On the first day, I got lost in a construction area near Hemisfair Park and found myself in an underground grotto with no one around except shadows. This inspired the first chapter. Thankfully, I was in no danger.

After climbing the steps aboveground, a group of nurses attending a conference adopted me until I could get my bearings. I also wanted my characters to get some time to enjoy all the delicious food I experienced on the River Walk. Sadly, those pesky villains wouldn't allow it. Even thinking about it makes me crave some tableside guacamole.

I've had a lot of good times with the McGuire family. I'm glad all four brothers got a chance to find love. I hope from here on out, they can enjoy some family time without danger following them.

I love to hear from readers. Feel free to contact me through my website, WritingHeather.com. In addition, those who subscribe to my newsletter are occasionally given opportunities to receive advance reader copies of my books.

Blessings,
Heather Woodhaven

Get 2 Free Books,
Plus 2 Free Gifts—
just for trying the Reader Service!

Love Inspired

Get 2 Free Books,

Plus 2 Free Gifts—

just for trying the Reader Service!

YES! Please send me **The Hometown Hearts Collection** in Larger Print. This collection begins with 3 FREE books and 2 FREE gifts in the first shipment. Along with my 3 free books, I'll also get the next 4 books from the Hometown Hearts Collection, in LARGER PRINT, which I may either return and owe nothing, or keep for the low price of $4.99 U.S./ $5.89 CDN each plus $2.99 for shipping and handling per shipment*. If I decide to continue, about once a month for 8 months I will get 6 or 7 more books, but will only need to pay for 4. That means 2 or 3 books in every shipment will be FREE! If I decide to keep the entire collection, I'll have paid for only 32 books because 19 books are FREE! I understand that accepting the 3 free books and gifts places me under no obligation to buy anything. I can always return a shipment and cancel at any time. My free books and gifts are mine to keep no matter what I decide.

262 HCN 3432 462 HCN 3432

Name	(PLEASE PRINT)	
Address		Apt. #
City	State/Prov.	Zip/Postal Code

Signature (if under 18, a parent or guardian must sign)

Mail to the **Reader Service:**
IN U.S.A.: P.O. Box 1867, Buffalo, NY. 14240-1867
IN CANADA: P.O. Box 609, Fort Erie, Ontario L2A 5X3

* Terms and prices subject to change without notice. Prices do not include applicable taxes. Sales tax applicable in NY. Canadian residents will be charged applicable taxes. This offer is limited to one order per household. All orders subject to approval. Credit or debit balances in a customer's account(s) may be offset by any other outstanding balance owed by or to the customer. Please allow 4 to 6 weeks for delivery. Offer available while quantities last. Offer not available to Quebec residents.

Your Privacy—The Reader Service is committed to protecting your privacy. Our Privacy Policy is available online at www.ReaderService.com or upon request from the Reader Service.

We make a portion of our mailing list available to reputable third parties that offer products we believe may interest you. If you prefer that we not exchange your name with third parties, or if you wish to clarify or modify your communication preferences, please visit us at www.ReaderService.com/consumerchoice or write to us at Reader Service Preference Service, P.O. Box 9062, Buffalo, NY. 14240-9062. Include your complete name and address.

READERSERVICE.COM

Manage your account online!

- Review your order history
- Manage your payments
- Update your address

We've designed the Reader Service website just for you.

Enjoy all the features!

- Discover new series available to you, and read excerpts from any series.
- Respond to mailings and special monthly offers.
- Browse the Bonus Bucks catalog and online-only exculsives.
- Share your feedback.

Visit us at:

ReaderService.com

RS16R